This book belongs to

Bevan

Children's
POOLBEG

S.K.U.N.K. and the Splitting Earth

S.K.U.N.K. and the Splitting Earth

Children's
POOLBEG

A Paperback Original
First published 1991 by
Poolbeg Press Ltd
Knocksedan House,
Swords, Co Dublin, Ireland

Poolbeg Press receives financial assistance from the Arts
Council/An Chomhairle Ealaíon, Ireland

ISBN 1 85371 119 5

Cover design by Steven Hope
Set by Richard Parfrey
Printed by Guernsey Press Limited
Vale Guernsey Channel Islands

Also available from Children's Poolbeg

S.K.U.N.K. and the Ozone Conspiracy
by
Margrit Cruickshank

"A good fast-moving story…exciting, humorous
and very well written."

Books Ireland

To Woolworth

"But he is a very fine cat, a very fine cat indeed."

Samuel Johnson

Contents

1
Earthquakes and Volcanoes

ANIC AS EARTH MOVES AGAIN! The headline caught Aisling Daly's eye as she cycled past the newsagents on Dalkey's main street. There must have been another earthquake somewhere. They were happening practically every day now: everyone was blaming the greenhouse effect or the ozone holes—except her godfather Seamus. As usual, he'd refused to tell her anything.

She looked at her watch: 5.45. With any luck, John Smith's bookshop would still be open. If anyone—apart from Seamus—would know what was happening, it was John Smith. He *said* he'd retired from the British Secret Service when they'd come back from fighting S.K.U.N.K. in Switzerland almost a year ago, but she didn't believe him. She was sure his bookshop in Dalkey was only a cover for his real work—anyone with a name like John Smith *had* to be a spy.

She leant her bike against the sill of the shop's old-fashioned bow window and went in. It was empty. Through the frosted glass which screened the office from the main part of the shop, she could just make out two figures. Rats, she thought: he was obviously busy with a customer. She would have to wait.

She browsed through the boxes of second-hand books, her fingers becoming floury with grey dust: *Love among the Ashes*, *The Mystery of the Stuffed Guinea-pig*, *Six Hundred Ways to Knit a Sock*.

Someone came out of the office. It was a small, balding, shy-looking man wearing large spectacles with heavy black frames. He looked a bit like a startled owl, she thought. He raised his hat as he passed her. "Hi, kid. Find anything interesting, reading-wise?"

Before she had time to answer, he had moved on. He stopped just short of the bow window and peered cautiously out over a display of second-hand encyclopaedias. Aisling looked out as well, but could see nothing unusual. The man opened the door abruptly, scurried through it and dashed behind a group of passing pedestrians.

John Smith appeared beside her. "Evening, Aisling. What brings you here? If you're looking for something to improve your mind, you'd better hurry up. It's nearly closing time."

She put down the book she was holding: *How to Get Fit on Bread, Bacon and Bananas.* "Who was that?" she asked, nodding towards the door.

He shrugged. "A seeker after knowledge, like yourself. I didn't, however, ask him for references. Should I have done?"

"He was acting very suspiciously. What did he want?"

John Smith looked at her. "I could say it was none of your business. But then, who am I to discourage the curiosity of the young? He was interested in vulcanology, if you really want to know. Called after Vulcanos, also known as Volcanos, the Roman god of fire—as any good encyclopaedia will tell you."

Aisling groaned. John Smith had pretended to sell encyclopaedias when he'd worked for MI5—he never missed a chance to show off his knowledge.

"I take it you mean he's studying volcanoes," she said sarcastically.

"Congratulations. Seamus would be delighted to hear that they do teach you something in school nowadays. Now, can I get you a book? It's nearly six o'clock and I want to go home."

"I just wanted to check something and the library's closed," Aisling explained. "It closes at 5.30 on Fridays."

"I am aware of that. And so should you be. If you were still at school, I suppose there'd be some excuse; but I can't help thinking it smacks of carelessness not to manage to get to a library before closing time in the summer holidays. I'm also not sure I approve of being regarded as a second-best public library service. Still, now you're here, what do you want to know."

"Do you have anything on earthquakes?"

John Smith rubbed his chin. "First volcanoes and now earthquakes. I wonder why."

"It's topical. Everyone's talking about them. I want to find out more."

"Very laudable. (From the Latin *laudare*: to praise, meaning therefore 'praiseworthy,' as any good encyclopedia would tell you.) Only I don't think that's the whole truth."

"Well, no..." Aisling hesitated. "You see, Mum's discovered the larder's damp and the jam's beginning to go mouldy so she's dumping it on everyone. You'll probably get a jar yourself—everyone in South County Dublin seems to be getting one. And she asked me to take a couple of jars to Florence and Seamus this afternoon."

John Smith smiled. "Thanks for the warning. Go on."

"Well...when I got to Florence's, Seamus was working on one of his big canvasses. And he was painting an earthquake."

John Smith was silent or a minute. Then: "Did he say why?"

"You know Seamus." Aisling grinned. 'I am painting an earthquake because it is more aesthetically pleasing and compositionally demanding than a hunk of stale cheese. And because it's Monday—or not, as the case may be. Why do YOU think I'm painting an earthquake, child?' She mimicked Seamus's testy voice.

"So you came here?" John Smith looked guarded.

"Yes. Well, actually, I thought maybe you would know what's going on."

"Hmm." He drummed his fingers thoughtfully on the back of a copy of *Ulysses*. "I thought Seamus knew more than he admitted," he said, half to himself. "Maybe I'd better pay him another visit."

"Then there is something going on! I knew I was right!" Aisling looked at her watch. "Mum's expecting me at six. Can't we go after dinner? Or tomorrow afternoon?—I'm not doing anything then."

"You can go when you like. I don't remember suggesting you come with me."

"That's not fair! I was a great help last time, wasn't I? You'd never have got the prism to Hermann in Switzerland without me."

"Life is unfair. As you'll find in the encyclopaedia under A for Aphorisms, otherwise known as wise sayings. And this time is different. If there is a 'this time' at all. You run along now and let me shut up shop."

Rats, thought Aisling as she cycled home. That was absolutely typical. Both Seamus and John Smith had been happy enough to have her along last year, when they'd needed her. And now they were both treating her like a stupid little kid again. Well, if they weren't going to tell her anything, she'd have to find out herself. She'd go up to Seamus's after tea and see if she could trick him into giving her a hint as to what was going on. Then she'd follow it up herself and show them. She imagined the headlines in the *Irish Times*: *Schoolgirl solves mystery of recent spate of earth tremors!* To heck with John Smith and Seamus—she'd find out what all these earthquakes were about despite them both!

But she had to wait for the next day after all. She had been late for tea, despite cycling like mad from the bookshop, and then she'd fought with Kevin and argued with her dad and been sent to bed. She turned on her transistor and listened to the news: earth tremors had been felt in California, in Turkey, in Italy and in central Scotland; a volcano in North America and Mount Etna in Sicily had erupted simultaneously. A scientist was interviewed who said it was natural for periods of intense seismological activity to occur every now and again: the earth, after all, had been changing shape for over two million years and was still doing so. Later, a member of the Church of the Last Judgement gave a talk on 'The End of the World' and claimed that God had finally lost patience with mankind: unless everybody joined his church NOW and gave a donation to the High Priest, c/ o Barclay's Bank, we would all be blown sky-high in the Final Celestial Explosion. Aisling switched off: she believed neither of them.

Early the next morning she cycled up to her godfather Seamus's house overlooking Dalkey Hill. His sister Florence opened the door. Her round pink face broke into a smile. "Aisling! I didn't expect to see you back so soon. Have you had breakfast?"

"Well, sort of."

"'I see. It's no wonder all you children are so wishy-washy looking. Come into the kitchen and I'll make you something proper to eat. Would you like sausage, bacon and eggs or would you prefer pancakes? I think I've got some maple syrup somewhere. And there's plenty of porridge, of course..."

Aisling was tempted but restrained herself: once you started eating Florence's cooking you could forget what you came for. "Thanks, but I want to see Seamus. Is he up yet?"

"Naturally. But he's got a lot on his mind. Perhaps I'd better ask first if he wants to see you."

Aisling followed her into the kitchen. She nibbled at one of the scones fresh from the oven, which were cooling on the table, while Florence unhooked a speaking tube from beside the sink and whistled into it. She held it away from her ear and waited.

Mulligan, her immense orange cat, was lying sprawled across a kitchen chair, his tail falling down one side of it and his front paws and head over the other. He looked fast asleep. But no sooner had Aisling's teeth bitten into the warm crust of the scone than he was off the chair, which fell with a clatter behind him, and was sitting begging on his hind legs in front of her. She grinned at him and gave him a piece of scone. "Honest, Mulligan. You're the greediest cat I know."

Seamus's voice came through the speaking tube. "Yes?"

"Aisling's here. She wants to see you."

There was a silence.

"Ask him again," Aisling whispered.

Florence shook her head. She returned the tube to its hook and picked up a dishcloth.

"All right." The speaking tube had suddenly come to life again. "Send her up."

Aisling went up two flights of stairs to the attic which her godfather, being confined to bed for a reason no one had ever explained and she'd always been too embarrassed to ask about, used both as a bedroom and a studio. Seamus was an artist and an inventor and his room was full of paintings, art materials and various gadgets which helped him organise his—and every one else's—life.

She paused for breath outside the studio door and knocked. "Come in," growled Seamus.

Aisling opened the door. As she did so, an orange streak thundered up the stairs behind her and flashed past her legs.

"And keep that rapacious omnivore out of here!"

She tried to grab Mulligan, missed and sprawled onto the carpet, crashing into a strange machine full of rolls of white paper like outsize toilet rolls. Mulligan disappeared under Seamus's bed.

"Watch the seismograph, child!" roared Seamus who was sitting up in his huge brass bed, glaring angrily at her.

She picked herself up and pulled the machine back to where it had been before she'd hit it. It was very heavy. She looked at it more closely. Seamus's studio was always full of machines: he had a machine to open the window, a machine to close the door, machines to brew cups of tea, sweep the room, operate the lift to the kitchen... But this machine was new. She tried to remember what a seismograph did. She was sure she'd heard the word before. She thought back to her science classes...

"Hmph." There was an angry grunt from the bed. "Did nobody teach you any manners, child? And shut that door!"

"Sorry," Aisling grinned. "Good morning, Seamus. How are you, Seamus? I hope you're keeping well, Seamus." She turned and shut the door quietly.

Seamus grunted. "That's better. But don't push your luck. And in future, I'd be obliged if you didn't start a conversation with a rugby tackle on the nearest piece of furniture. Well?"

"Sorry."

"I take it you came here for a reason? Or do you find my company so enthralling that you have to see me every day?"

"No. I mean, yes. I mean..."

"Stop mumbling and tell me what you want. I happen to be busy, believe it or not."

"I saw John Smith yesterday," Aisling began.

"So?"

"He said he was coming here."

"And?"

"He was going to ask you about earthquakes."

"Was he?" Seamus raised a bushy eyebrow. "I would have thought that if anyone knew everything there was to know about earthquakes it was that walking encyclopaedia of a bookseller."

"Didn't he come, then?" asked Aisling in surprise.

"Did I say he didn't? Will you get to the point, child?"

"I'd like to know what's going on!" said Aisling, exasperated.

"What makes you think anything at all is going on, as you put it?"

Aisling looked straight at him. "There's all these earthquakes and volcanoes and earth tremors and everything everywhere recently and you were painting an earthquake yesterday and John Smith was coming here to talk about earthquakes…something must be going on."

"Hmph." Seamus doodled a volcano on the sketch pad on his knees. "I'm inclined to agree with you. But what?"

"Don't you know?"

"I know what I read in the papers. Though I must admit I have my suspicions."

Aisling waited expectantly for Seamus to say more. As the silence lengthened she became aware of a strange noise under the bed: a sort of rattling sound, as if a small metal object was being knocked about on the floor. She hoped it wasn't an open tube of paint. Mulligan had attacked one of these before, a tube of *crimson lake*, in fact: the carpet still looked as if someone had once been murdered on it.

Suddenly a small round object shot out from under the bed. It lay, rocking back and forth for a minute, just beside Aisling's foot, and then Mulligan pounced, landed on it, fell over on his side, grasped it with his front paws and tried to kick its belly open with his back claws, let it go, moved back, crouched, wriggled his backside and pounced again, this time swiping it across the room to the skirting board. He chased after it, caught it in his paws, threw it in the air, jumped onto it, batted it back towards the bed and crouched behind a chair, his ears flat, his eyes huge, his tail lashing and his hips wriggling, daring it to fight back. When it wouldn't, he sprang at it again and knocked it back under the bed. He followed it back in and there was silence again.

Aisling expected Seamus to explode: after all, she'd had no business letting Mulligan into the studio at all. She hoped it wasn't anything particularly valuable he'd found to play with, especially as the rumbling noises had resumed under the bed.

But Seamus just looked thoughtful.

"You were going to tell me about earthquakes," she reminded him.

Seamus didn't reply. He picked up his pen and started to write on the sketch pad in front of him.

"There must be something going on," Aisling insisted. "Why don't you..."

Seamus looked up and put a finger to his lips. He turned the paper he'd been writing on towards her so that she could see what he had written.

She read: WATCH IT! THAT WAS A MICROPHONE. WE HAVE BEEN BUGGED.

2
Bugged

"I want you to post a letter for me," Seamus said calmly. "Just be quiet for a minute while I finish it."

Aisling peered under the bed but Mulligan had retreated to the far side of it. Could it really be a microphone he had in his paws?

Seamus wrote some more words on the paper. "Here. Take this to the postbox on the corner." He handed it to her. On it was written: *Go down to the road and see if you can see a van or a lorry. Whoever's listening must be parked not too far away.*

"D'you mean...?'

"Stop arguing and do as you're told." Seamus put a finger to his lips and pointed down under his bed.

"Oh. Of course."

Aisling raced downstairs and burst out onto the road. It was quiet. There were one or two cars parked opposite the entrance to Dalkey Park, but she could see from the gate that they were empty. A stray dog came across and cocked his leg against the gatepost; a few children were knocking a football about on the grass below the car park; and, a good bit down the road to her left, there was a white van. That had to be it. She walked towards it. As she got nearer, she could see lettering on its side: KLEENALL LAUNDRY

She walked past it. There was no-one in the driving cab. She went round to the back of the van and listened—if someone was inside the van monitoring the microphone, they weren't making a noise. Without giving herself time to change her mind, she rapped on the door. There was no answer.

She looked round carefully. No-one was watching. Taking a deep breath, she tried the handle. The door was unlocked. Very gently, she started to pull it open.

The van was practically empty. There were a few packets of clean laundry and two bags of dirty laundry near the door but, if there was anyone there, listening to Seamus's conversations, Aisling had to admit he'd have to be the size of a mouse. So who had planted the microphone?

She looked up and down the road again but there was definitely no other vehicle. She shrugged and went back to Seamus's house. Seamus was getting old and his eyesight was probably fading. She hadn't looked at the thing Mulligan was playing with properly—it could have been anything, she told herself. She shut the gate behind her and turned to go back inside.

As she did so, a movement from the house next door caught her eye. She looked up. The net curtain swung back into place across an upstairs window but she had seen a face she recognized: the thin owlish face with dark-rimmed glasses of the man who'd been talking to John Smith at the bookshop!

She rushed upstairs to Seamus's studio. "You were right!" she shouted. "It's.."

"Shhh!" He glared at her and put a paint-stained finger to his lips. She remembered the microphone and blushed. "Don't break my eardrums, child," Seamus said clearly, giving her a wink. "Just because *your* generation is making itself deaf on loud music, doesn't mean the rest of us have defective hearing. As for being right, I should hope I was—I may be stuck in this room, but I do know where the nearest post box is. Now, crawl under the bed and see what that misguided feline has mistaken for a mouse. I am fed up with lying on top of a hunting party."

Aisling grinned and crawled obediently under the bed. She found a lot of dust, a couple of tubes of paint, three paint brushes, a ruler, a biro, some peas shrivelled into bullet-hard pellets, Mulligan (whose tail, lashing gently, was creating a miniature dust-storm around him) and the small round microphone.

She picked it up gingerly and crawled back out from under the bed. She showed it silently to Seamus.

"Chuck it down the stairs, child," he suggested. "That fat orange lump can do with some exercise."

"Come on, Mulligan." Aisling whistled loudly into the microphone. She hoped that the ears of the thin owlish man listening next door were hurting. She rubbed the microphone back and forth across the carpet to entice Mulligan out. He watched her for a minute, his eyes huge and black, his tail lashing; and then he shot out from under the bed like a furry torpedo. She withdrew the microphone at the last second, opened the door, caught Mulligan's attention again by banging the mike against the door jamb, and flung it down the stairs.

Mulligan leapt after it, knocking it from step to step and banging it up against the wall. He dribbled it across the landing and then pursued it helter-skelter down the bottom flight of stairs to the street door. If anyone was listening, they ought to be half-deaf by now, Aisling thought with satisfaction. She returned to the studio.

"Well? You were going to tell me what's going on."

"Earthquakes. And volcanoes. I thought you'd noticed."

"You know what I mean. Why are they happening?"

"Because the tectonic plates are moving apart or because it's Monday or—if you believe that idiot on the box yesterday—because the end of the world is at hand. Why do you think they're happening?"

Aisling hesitated. "I don't know. I thought it might have been S.K.U.N.K. again. You know, the gang that tried to blackmail the world last year by making a hole in the ozone layer. It seems the sort of thing they'd do—if we hadn't destroyed their headquarters and they weren't all locked up in jail, I would have bet anything it was them."

Seamus grunted. "Take my advice, child: never bet. And especially not on something as slippery as our friends in S.K.U.N.K. They're like a worm: cut a bit off, the rest survives. Or like a lizard when you chop its tail off. People like that go on for ever."

"Do you think S.K.U.N.K. really is organising the earthquakes, then?"

Seamus looked thoughtful. "It wouldn't surprise me. And from what John Smith didn't say when he was up last night, I should think the possibility struck him too."

"But how on earth are they doing it? You can't just make an earthquake, can you?"

"There's certainly more to it than boiling an egg. But it's not impossible. You should know by now that the mind of man is capable of anything—and that he usually uses it for evil rather than good."

Aisling tried a different approach. "What are we going to do about it, then?"

"We?"

"How are we going to stop them?"

"*We*, child, are not going to stop them. It would appear that John Smith is going to get the British Navy to do that." Seamus didn't sound pleased. "It's just as well we don't have more ships in our own navy or he'd have *them* steaming about all over the North Atlantic too."

Aisling thought about this. "Oh," she said. "I'd hoped…"

"No doubt. Now, would you please get out of here. I am expecting a visitor and I have work to do."

"Can't we at least try something?"

"No." Seamus glared at her. "Goodbye."

Reluctantly, Aisling stood up to go. She heard footsteps bounding up the stairs. She waited. The door opened and an untidy young man burst into the room. His curly black hair was tied back with an elastic band, his sweater was so full of holes her mother would have put it straight in the bin, and the rips in his jeans were fixed together with, she noticed with an appreciative grin, nappy pins. He flung himself down into the chair beside the bed and stared at the skylight with a rapt expression.

"Well?" Seamus demanded.

"Definitely!" He removed his gaze from the skylight and smiled happily. "Isn't life terrific!"

"Did you find anything out, boy? Was I right?"

"Well…" The young man blushed and avoided

Seamus's eye. "I...it was very difficult. We did have a little talk, but she was very busy."

"She?"

"My contact."

"Hmmm."

"I'm seeing her again tomorrow, though," the young man added hastily. "I'll ask her then."

Seamus glared at him. "You'll ask her now. Tomorrow may be too late. Maybe you'd better take Aisling here with you, seeing as how she doesn't seem to know when she's not wanted. She might manage to make you keep your mind on what you're supposed to be doing this time. I want to know where the epicentre is."

"The what?" Aisling asked.

"Look it up when you get home." He glared at the young man. "There's been far too much time wasted already. If S.K.U.N.K. is behind this, we'll have to act fast."

"Skunk?" asked the young man. "Who's Skunk?"

"A gang of megalomaniacs no nice young person should have anything to do with. Now, are you going to get out of here or do I have to throw you out?"

"Come on." The young man pulled Aisling towards the door. "When he's in a mood, there's no sense in arguing."

"In a mood, is it? Why, you insolent young whippersnapper...!"

The young man shut the door just as something hit the other side of it. "I'm Chris," he said. "I gather you're Aisling. I'm supposed to be writing an article about Seamus for this art magazine, but every time I try to interview him, he finds something else for me to do. At this rate I'll be as old as he is before I finish it."

Aisling grinned. "We'd better get going to wherever it is we're going to then, so that you can get back and start again. Where is it we're supposed to be going?"

"Merrion Square. You don't have a lid, do you?"

Aisling looked at him blankly.

"A helmet. No, obviously not. Well, I'm not taking you without one."

"D'you mean a motorcycle helmet?" Aisling had never been on a motorbike. *Heavy Metaller Aisling Daly roars off to mug old ladies!* she thought with a grin. "I'll ask Florence. You never know what she can come up with."

Florence was at the sink peeling potatoes as they came into the kitchen. She looked up. "So you're back, Christopher. Is she coming to lunch?"

Chris went bright red. "No," he said dreamily. "I asked, but she was too busy."

'Who?" asked Aisling.

Mulligan had followed them downstairs and was now gazing, equally dreamily, at the pot on the stove. Chris tickled him absent-mindedly under the chin. Mulligan arched his back and purred.

Aisling looked at Florence, who winked back at her. She smiled. "I've no idea, child. He has a different girl every time I see him."

Chris blushed even more. "I'll wait for you outside, Aisling," he muttered and left quickly.

"Oh, is that all." Aisling was disappointed. "You don't have a motor cycle helmet anywhere, do you Florence?"

Florence smiled and patted her white sausage-like curls into place. She opened the door of a tall cupboard beside the fridge. At the back of the door hung her crossbow and a quiver of bolts, and on one of the shelves facing them was a silver motorcycle helmet with a black eagle painted on the front. She handed it to Aisling. "There, try that. I think it should fit you."

Aisling stared at it in amazement. You really never knew what Florence would come up with next. "Who is Chris?" she asked as she strapped the helmet under her chin.

"Christopher?" Florence smiled. "Christopher is in love."

"Yuk," said Aisling. "Who with?"

"Anyone who takes his fancy. We've known him four weeks now and I've lost count of the number of girls he's fallen in love with. He is also hoping to become a journalist, which is why he's bothering your godfather."

"He's not an ex-convict like Dermot was?" Aisling couldn't resist asking mischievously.

"Certainly not. And it's not like you to be nasty about poor Dermot. He may have been easily led, poor boy—he certainly let these nasty men, Shavitov and Lerntowski, take him in. But I'm sure he has learnt his lesson and you know he had a heart of gold."

Aisling gave Florence a hug. "Of course he had," she agreed. A motorbike horn tooted outside. "I'll have to go. Give Dermot my regards next time you write to him."

"Of course." Florence took a tiny lace-edged handkerchief out of the pocket of her pinny and blew her nose. "Just tell that young man to drive carefully."

3
Frankie

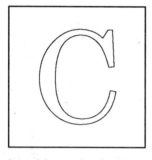

hris was waiting for her outside Seamus's front gate. She climbed up behind him, he kicked the starting pedal and the bike took off with a roar.

She shut her eyes and clung to him in terror, burying her face in his black leather jacket and letting the ear-shattering noise rush over her and the wind whistle past at what seemed like a hundred miles an hour. She could see why Florence had suggested she tell Chris to drive carefully, only it was a bit too late now, she thought grimly. She imagined her parents reading the headlines in the evening paper: *Talented Irish schoolgirl killed in motorbike crash!* She hoped it wouldn't hurt too much.

Gradually she became used to the noise and

the speed and dared to open her eyes again. They weren't actually going that fast, she realized. And if they'd come this far safely, no doubt they'd be okay. By the time they had roared through Dun Laoghaire and Blackrock, she was almost enjoying herself.

Chris stopped in Merrion Square. He parked the bike against some railings and bounded up a flight of granite steps to a solid wooden door with a Georgian fanlight over it. Taking off her silver helmet, Aisling followed him. On the door was a plate with the words:

INSTITIÚID ÁRD-LEINN BHAILE ÁTHA CLIATH
DUBLIN INSTITUTE FOR ADVANCED STUDIES
SCHOOL OF COSMIC PHYSICS

Chris pushed open the door and led her down to the basement. He stopped in front of a white-painted door, pushed a strand of hair which had escaped from the elastic band back over his ear, pulled his jumper straight, brushed a couple of Mulligan's hairs off his jeans, took a deep breath and went in.

Aisling followed him into a small office. Beyond it was a laboratory full of machines and scientific equipment. Through the open door she could see a seismograph like the one she'd nearly knocked over in Seamus's studio.

The office was full of people: two men and a woman in white laboratory coats, one large fat man in a shiny blue suit, one army officer, one naval officer and—Aisling stiffened—an owlish little man with a felt hat and glasses. How, if he'd been watching Seamus's house in Dalkey, had he got here before them? She thought back. Neither Seamus nor Chris had mentioned where she and Chris were going— she'd only found out herself when they'd arrived at the door. Was it a coincidence? Or had he followed them and somehow guessed where they were heading and overtaken them at the last minute? She stared at him. He looked back, raised his hat and smiled.

She suddenly became aware that the atmosphere in the room was so unfriendly it would have made even Santa Claus turn round and go back up the chimney: everyone was glaring at her and Chris as if they were TV licence snoopers.

"What is the meaning of this?" snapped the man in the shiny blue suit. "I thought this was a confidential meeting?"

The woman looked at Chris and raised a

beautifully shaped eyebrow.

"Er..." Chris went scarlet again.

She turned to the others. "Excuse me, gentlemen. I won't be a minute. You carry on, Aidan."

She ushered Chris and Aisling back into the corridor and shut the door. Then she turned on Chris: "What on earth are you doing here now? I told you I had an important conference today." Her green eyes flashed angrily and her chestnut hair swung forwards across her high cheekbones. Chris stared at her open-mouthed, like a dog begging to be taken for a walk.

"Did I tell you how beautiful she is, Ash?" he asked hoarsely. "Especially when she's angry. She's like a dream, a filmstar, a goddess!"

"Get out!" ordered the goddess. "Go away!"

Chris practically wagged his tail. It was only when she turned to go back into the room that he woke from his trance. He pulled her away from the door. "I've got to speak to you, Frankie."

She looked at him as if he was a postage stamp folded in four. "Have you gone mad? Are you trying to lose me my job? I am supposed to be leading a conference in there, in case it had escaped your notice. Let me go."

"Please, Frankie!" Chris still held her arm. "I have to see you now. It's very urgent. Tomorrow may be too late. We have to know where the earthquakes are coming from."

"We?" Frankie asked coldly.

"Seamus O'Toole told me to find out. You know, the artist. He thinks that someone's causing all this seismic movement and, if he finds out where it's coming from, he'll try to stop it. If anyone can, he can, Frankie."

Frankie looked at him closely. "You may be an idiot, Chris my love. But you're honest, I'll give you that. And I've met Seamus. I agree with you, my sweet, he's quite something."

"Well then. Can you tell us what's going on?"

She hesitated for a minute, then shrugged. "What's so secret about it, anyway? Everyone knows what's happening, after all."

"What is happening?" asked Aisling. "And where are the earthquakes coming from?"

"Iceland," said Frankie. "That's been obvious for some time. But it just didn't seem possible. At first we thought it was natural, just the earth settling down a bit more: after all, the continents are still drifting. And then we realized that it was more than just normal movement of the earth's crust. Something strange was happening. And then...I'm not sure if I should tell you..."

"Go on," said Chris and Aisling together.

"Well, no doubt it'll be common news soon—but you'd better keep it under your hats for the meantime: the big powers all got a message. Someone in Iceland is controlling all these earthquakes and tremors and they have threatened to make things worse. They could wipe out half the cities in the world."

"Unless?" Aisling asked.

"I'm not sure what they threatened. That's one thing the gentlemen in there won't tell a mere scientist like myself. What they want to know is where the enemy is so that they can destroy him. Or them, more likely."

"How?"

Frankie shrugged. "How should I know? Bomb Iceland to smithereens, I would say. And to heck with all the seals and gerfalcons and puffins and auks and what-have-you."

"And people," said Chris, coming out of his trance.

"Exactly, my sweet," said Frankie. "So we're trying to pinpoint the precise location of the start of the shock waves. I'd love to know how they get them to travel where they like underground and then come up just where they want them. I wish I knew just who was working on that project and how they've achieved it. It's a major breakthrough in geo-science..."

The door opened and the technician Frankie had called Aidan stuck his head out. "Are you finished?" he asked. "The brass in here are getting restless."

"Just coming," said Frankie. She shook herself free of Chris's hand. "Go home now like a good boy," she said. "I'll see you tomorrow."

"Where is the exact location?" Aisling asked quickly.

"We think it's near Snaefellsjökul, a glacier on the west coast. Now, *go!*" Frankie kissed Chris quickly on the cheek, smiled at Aisling and went back to the conference.

Chris touched his cheek with reverent fingers and stared dreamily at the closed door. Aisling had practically to drag him away. "Rats!" she exclaimed suddenly as they reached the stairs. "That man. Owl-face. I forgot to ask her what he was doing in there." She started to go back down the corridor.

Chris stopped her. "Come on, Ash. No point in annoying her again—she mightn't forgive us as quickly next time. We'd better get back and tell Seamus."

"But he's a spy!" Aisling said urgently. "We have to warn Frankie."

"Who's a spy?"

"That man with the glasses. Owl-face. He was spying on Seamus just before you came. We found his microphone. He bugged Seamus's studio."

"What on earth are you burbling on about? Nobody spies nowadays—it's gone out of fashion." He saw the expression on her face. "Okay. If it's really worrying you, tell the man at the information desk upstairs. But don't go back and annoy Frankie now. All right?"

Aisling had to be content with that. She felt a fool muttering on about spies to the elderly academic-looking gentleman at the desk upstairs, but he courteously wrote down her message and promised to deliver it to Frankie. It was the best she could do. She wondered if Owl-face belonged to S.K.U.N.K. Seamus had hinted that they might be behind the earthquakes and things. After S.K.U.N.K.'s headquarters had been destroyed and the whole gang had been arrested last year, she'd thought that that was the last they'd hear from them. But if Shavitov and Lerntowski had escaped... She shivered. It'd be just like them to hold the world to ransom once again!

4
Drifting Continents

ell?" Seamus asked when they returned to the studio.

"The epicentre's in Iceland," said Chris. "In this place called Snaefells-something, Frankie thinks. I thought Snaefells was a mountain on the Isle of Man?"

"And Dublin's in at least seven states in the USA. So what?"

"The governments have all got blackmail letters," Aisling said. "You were right: it must be S.K.U.N.K. again. We've got to stop them."

"So you keep telling me. It's not like stopping the No 8 bus, child. S.K.U.N.K. are a nasty lot. I'm surprised you want to tangle with them again."

Aisling remembered the S.K.U.N.K. agents who had captured her in Switzerland. She shuddered. And yet... "All right, I was scared a lot of the time," she admitted. "But I was a lot of use too, wasn't I?"

"If we're being honest, I suppose I'll have to agree with you. Even that damn cat—which I see you've let in again—was worth his weight in raw liver. Which is saying something."

Mulligan, aware that he was being talked about, jumped onto the bed and spread his vast form across Seamus's stomach. Seamus scowled but let him be.

"Do you want to use my plane?" Chris asked.

"*Your* plane? Can you fly?" One of Aisling's secret hopes was that one day her parents might win the lottery and she'd have enough money to learn to fly. *Air ace Aisling Daly stuns the crowd at Baldonnel with her sensational aerobatic display!*

"He won a plane in a raffle along with a course of flying lessons. I don't know what the world is coming to," Seamus grumbled. "And he didn't answer your question. Can you fly?"

"Well, yes." Chris smiled modestly. "A bit."

"Enough to get us to Iceland?"

Chris looked doubtfully at Seamus's huge brass bed. "I could certainly get the plane there, but you'll have to get out of that bed—

there's no way it would fit in. It's not a jumbo jet, you know."

"Huh." Seamus looked thoughtful. "Pass me the atlas there, child. Let's see just where this place is. Snaefells... Aha! It could be either a peninsula called Snaefellsness due north of Reykjavik, or an extinct volcano called Snaefellsjökul right at the end of it." He scratched his chin with a pencil. "Snaefellsjökul," he repeated. "Where have I heard that name before?"

"Wasn't that the place they started from in Jules Verne's *Journey to the Centre of the Earth*?" Aisling suggested. Seamus raised an eyebrow. "Surprising source of information you are sometimes, Aisling. Maybe the education system nowadays isn't quite as bad as I thought. And I believe you're right. In which cases it seems particularly apt that S.K.U.N.K., if it is S.K.U.N.K., are using it now. An extinct volcano...I wonder why." Aisling waited impatiently as Seamus scribbled volcano shapes on the pad in front of him. Then he drew a rough map of the Atlantic, with North America on one side and Europe on the other. He put Iceland between the two and drew a hard black line right through the island and down the centre of the Atlantic

Ocean. "The mid-Atlantic fault," he said thoughtfully. "That would make sense. But how are they doing it? That is the question."

"Frankie wondered that too," Aisling said. She looked at Seamus's map. "What did you say that line was?"

Seamus sighed. "I knew that last bit of intelligence was a flash in the pan. Have you never heard of the mid-Atlantic fault, child? Don't they teach you *any* basic geography in school?"

"They teach us a lot. But I've never heard of the mid-Atlantic whatsits. Is it important?"

"You explain it, Christopher. I'm thinking."

Chris took the sketch pad and removed a blank page. He tore this into various shapes which he placed on the top of the atlas Seamus had left balanced on Mulligan's broad back. "Okay, Ash. Are you sitting comfortably? Then we'll begin." Aisling groaned. Chris smiled sweetly. "Long, long ago, when the world was very young..."

"Get on with it."

"The land was squashed together in one corner of the globe, a bit like this." He fitted the torn pieces of paper together like an untidy jigsaw. "Okay. Now, in the course of a few billion years, all the continents started to move apart. North America—this piece here—drifted up and out to the left. South America followed it. This piece—Europe and Asia—moved north. Africa and India moved north after them. And you're left with Antarctica and Australia at the bottom."

Mulligan's tail began to lash. He stood up, knocking the atlas and the pieces of paper to the floor, shook himself like a terrier just out of the water, jumped off the bed, gave Chris a filthy look through narrowed eyes and collapsed half-way across the atlas on the carpet.

Seamus grinned. "So much for your geography lesson, boy. Will you get to the point We haven't got all day."

Chris ignored him. "Do you follow so far, Ash?"

"I knew all that already—we did it at school." She thought back to her geography lessons with Mr Langran: he had once muttered something about continental drift (she remembered having this vision of huge chunks of land floating about on top of the sea like bubble bath foam in the bath, colliding and drifting apart as you stirred your toes about); but all that was way before the dinosaurs even. "It all happened billions of years ago. I can't see why it's so important now."

"That's where you're wrong. As Frankie said this morning, the continents are still drifting. California, for example, is going to split off from America one of these days, geologically speaking, and float off into the Pacific Ocean; and India is still moving northwards and pushing the Himalayas up a bit every year."

"So if you're thinking of climbing Mount Everest, do it quickly," Seamus commented drily.

"Thanks," said Aisling. She turned back to Chris. "What about the line Seamus was muttering on about? The mid-Atlantic fault, or whatever it was."

"I was not muttering on, child. I never mutter on."

"Sorry." Aisling didn't sound it.

Chris sighed and pushed his fringe out of his eyes. "I was coming to that. A fault is where the various land masses come together— the joins of the jigsaw, so to speak. They can either be moving towards each other, as with India and Asia, and so make huge mountain ridges like the Himalayas; or they can be sliding apart like the mid-Atlantic fault which runs, as you can see from Seamus's drawing, right down the middle of the Atlantic Ocean under the sea. The land masses on either side of it are moving away from each other and new land, so to speak, is pushing up through the ocean floor to fill in the gap."

"Otherwise you'd have the whole Atlantic draining away like a gigantic bathtub," commented Seamus helpfully.

"This is bad enough to explain as it is, without you butting in all the time," objected Chris crossly. "Where was I?"

"The Atlantic was splitting down the middle," Aisling reminded him.

"Yes. So Africa and Europe are moving, very gradually, to the east; and America is moving, also very, very slowly, to the west. Still with me?"

"Sort of. Is that what you meant when you said California's going to fall off into the Pacific one day?"

"Exactly. Only, if someone manages to split the fault much faster, which is what S.K.U.N.K. appears to be doing, it'll all happen *now* rather than in the next few hundred thousand years. America will crash into the Pacific fault and the west coast, including San Francisco and my cousin John, will either blow up with eruptions from volcanoes or split apart with earthquakes and crash into the sea. As for

Europe, if it's pushed any faster to the east, we'll have the whole Mediterranean area, which is on another fault line, destroyed by volcanoes and earthquakes. Even small faults, where the surface of the earth is weak, will be in trouble. Like the Scottish Rift Valley between Glasgow and Edinburgh. So every country around the North Atlantic is threatened. And the split could extend into the South Atlantic too, with equally disastrous results. It's a fantastic plan!"

"I'm glad you've got back to the subject at last." Seamus tore off the page he'd been doodling on, crunched it up with his fingers and threw it at the waste paper basket. Mulligan, whom Aisling had thought was asleep, leapt up and pounced on it, landing head-first in the basket himself. He sat up, looked surprised, and then curled himself round to fit the basket and went back to sleep.

"That cat needs its head examined. Now listen. Christopher, I want you to get your plane ready. We need to leave first thing tomorrow morning. Meanwhile, I shall phone my old friend Hansie in Reykjavik and see what I can find out."

"What about me?" asked Aisling.

"You can hand me the phone."

Aisling bit back the remark she was tempted to make and passed him the telephone. He dialled 114. "Hello. Yes. I'd like to call a number in Iceland. No, *Ice*land. I...C...E... Thank you." He put his hand over the receiver. "Why do I always get the resident moron?" he asked. "Yes? Why not? Say that again, slowly. Well, what do you think it is? Typical." And he slammed the receiver back into its rest.

Aisling looked at Chris. He shrugged his shoulders.

"Did you get through?" she asked.

"No," said Seamus slowly. "Iceland can't be got. They've had all sorts of people trying to get through, but they haven't managed to make contact with anywhere in Iceland since yesterday. I wonder..." He looked at Chris. "Maybe you'd better go up yourself right now. Find out what you can and come straight back. I'll be organised by then."

"Do you have any idea how far it is?" asked Chris. "It's not just a matter of nipping down to Dalkey for a packet of crisps."

"It's about eight hundred miles as the crow flies. Certainly not more than a thousand. Just pretend you're a crow. Now move—this is urgent."

"Can I go with him?" Aisling asked quickly.

"Please!"

Seamus frowned. "Oh, all right then. Maybe you'll be able to keep his mind on what he's supposed to be doing." Aisling couldn't believe her ears. "I suppose you expect me to phone your mother and tell her you're spending the night here," Seamus went on. "Only don't go getting into trouble: I don't want to find myself explaining to your parents why you're feeding the polar bears in the arctic instead of being tucked up in bed downstairs. And, more importantly, I want you back here to report. Here's Hansie's address." He scribbled on a page from his notepad. "Find him, see if he's noticed anything unusual and then come straight back here. Right?"

"Right," said Chris. "Come on, Ash. Let's go."

5
Flight North

his time Aisling was much more relaxed about riding pillion on the motorbike and enjoyed the trip up to the airport. They stopped at a hangar at the end of the runway. Inside was a very small looking plane.

A mechanic jumped down from the wing and came towards them. He grinned. "She's A1, Chris. Running as smooth as a baby's bottom. Take you to hell and back, no trouble, she will."

Chris winked at Aisling. "She might have to. Roll her out, please, Phil, and get her ready for take off. I have to get clearance from Control. You wait here, Ash. I won't be a minute."

Phil taxied the plane out of the hangar and

44

parked it at the edge of the runway. "You going with him?" he asked.

"Yes." Aisling tried to sound casual about it. She was beginning to think she should have stayed at home. Somehow, she'd imagined Chris's plane would be normal, like the Aer Lingus jets she saw passing over Dalkey every day. She hadn't bargained on going off to Iceland in anything that looked as if it was tied together with pieces of string.

It was even worse once she was actually in the plane and they were speeding along the runway. She kept expecting Chris to lift its nose up into the air, but he just sat smiling calmly as they headed straight for the main Belfast road. She imagined the headlines in tomorrow's papers: *Horror as aeroplane crashes on to dual-carriageway!*

And then they were in the air and the airport was falling away behind them, the buildings looking like dolls' houses, the huge intercontinental jets waiting on the tarmac like tiny silverfish. She relaxed and began to enjoy herself.

The countryside passed underneath, a patchwork quilt chased over by cloud shadows which climbed hills and rushed across fields and darkened villages fleetingly as they passed.

The green, brown and yellow of County Louth gave way to the purple and brown of the Mourne mountains. Belfast appeared and disappeared on their right. Then they were over Lough Neagh and heading for the Antrim coast. And after that came the sea.

As Aisling looked down, its crests and troughs caught the sparkle of the sun and shattered it into a thousand glittering jewels. The islands of the Outer Hebrides passed on her right, each circled by a necklace of white spume; and then they left the land behind completely. Everywhere she looked, the sea stretched in an undulating mass to the horizon.

As they flew further and further north, Aisling felt more and more small and insignificant. She was glad when a line of ships appeared below them, black specks like a column of ants moving slowly northward. At least, if anything went wrong, there'd be someone to pick them up. *Daring rescue at sea: Irish schoolgirl relates her horrifying experiences...*

She heard Chris draw in his breath quickly. He leant forwards and examined one of the instruments on the panel in front of him. He tapped it urgently.

"Is anything the matter?"

He frowned, then forced a smile. "The compass has gone funny. But it's nothing to worry about."

"Does it matter?"

"Well, yes. In a way." He pushed his fringe back with nervous fingers. "I don't know about you, but I'd prefer not to miss Iceland and end up at the North Pole. Apart from anything else, Seamus wouldn't be too pleased."

"Are you sure we shouldn't turn back?" Aisling was conscious of a queasy feeling somewhere in the bottom of her stomach.

"Hold it a minute." He checked another instrument. "We've got enough fuel for quite a while yet. We'll go on a bit further. If we don't sight Iceland in the next half hour or so, we'll have to turn back anyway and refuel in Shetland."

Aisling tried to sound brave. "Seamus won't like that much."

"Damn Seamus. I'm not going to risk our lives. Okay?" Chris sounded rattled.

Aisling looked down again at the fleet of ships. The sea was empty—they must have passed over them already. She admitted to herself that Seamus had been right: being scared was no fun. "Do we have any parachutes?" she asked.

"Good thinking. There's no harm in being prepared—although we're not in any danger at all, yet."

Yet, thought Aisling as she found the parachutes, handed one to Chris and strapped the other on.

Chris gave her another not very convincing grin. "There we are, then. All set for every eventuality. Hey! What's that?"

The engine changed pitch and the plane started to vibrate alarmingly. It was if a giant had caught it in his huge hand and was shaking it up and down like a blocked salt cellar. Aisling looked at the instrument panel: the needles on the various dials were jumping about like drops of water on a red-hot plate. "What's the matter? What's happening?"

Chris ran his fingers through his hair again. "I don't know." He flicked a few knobs and pressed a few buttons. This only seemed to make things worse: the whole plane shook as if the giant had gone berserk: the wings juddered, the fuselage creaked and then the nose went down and the plane dived head first towards the sea.

Chris tugged at the controls. The engine shrieked. The sea rushed up to meet them. Aisling shut her eyes. She heard someone screaming but didn't realize it was herself...

At the very last minute the nose came up again. Aisling opened her eyes and let go of the seat she'd been clutching so hard her fingers had gone completely white. The sea was so close she felt she could have reached out and touched it—as it fell away again on their left she let out a breath she didn't know she'd been holding.

"What happened?" she asked, her voice trembling.

Chris was still having difficulty controlling the plane. "I don't know," he said grimly. "I can't risk it any longer."

As he spoke, a long strip of metal detached itself from the wing on Aisling's side and floated past her, glittering like a silver streamer in the sunshine. Chris pulled the plane round in a screaming curve.

The further south they got, the better the engine sounded and the less the plane shrieked and rattled, but it was still very far from right. Aisling stared ahead, wondering how far they were from Shetland and whether they'd make it. The wing beside her was like a tattered sleeve and more bits of metal were coming off it all the time.

Below her, she suddenly saw the flotilla of

ships they'd passed before. She breathed a sigh of relief: they didn't seem so helpless and alone now. She looked down again. Something funny was going on. She touched Chris's arm and pointed down. "What are they up to?" she asked.

Chris glanced at the sea below. The foremost ships were milling about in a large circle. Signals flashed from one to another like fairy lights. "I don't know," he said. The ships fell away behind them.

Then the tip of the wing on Aisling's side fell off. The plane veered suddenly and Chris struggled with the controls. The noise in the cockpit was shattering. Aisling watched, her mouth dry with terror, as Chris pulled the plane round and headed back north again to where the ships had been. The sea came closer and closer.

Chris spoke urgently into the mouthpiece of his headset: "Mayday! Mayday! We are in trouble. We will have to bale out. Can you pick us up?" He turned to Aisling. "Count five after you jump and pull the ring here. Got it?"

She nodded, her teeth chattering with fear.

He leant over her and opened the door. Then he undid her safety belt. "Okay? Now: *jump!*" The sea was very far away. She hesitated.

Before she realized what he was up to, Chris had pushed her out and she was falling through space. She looked down: the sea was rushing up to meet her, looking black and frightening. She pulled the ring as Chris had told her. There was a jerk and she stopped falling. Above her, the parachute billowed out against the blue sky. Below her, the sea was still getting near—not so quickly now, but still at an alarming rate. She heard an explosion behind her and, looking round quickly, she saw the plane crash into the sea. Before she could look for Chris's parachute, the sea was at her feet. Then she hit it. It was like jumping off the top board in the swimming pool, only the sea, despite the heat of summer, was freezing and she was not only fully-dressed, she was tangled up in the lines of her parachute as well. She came to the surface. spitting salty water. Fortunately, her legs were free and she was able to tread water. She wondered how long she could keep it up.

6
Allies

he woke to a noise she had heard before somewhere: the pounding of huge engines. It reminded her of something...

She opened her eyes. The lights were too bright and she shut them again quickly, but not before she had seen a face bending down over her. She opened her eyes again cautiously. Yes, she had been right—the face bending over her *was* John Smith's.

"What on earth are *you* doing here?"

He smiled cheerfully. "Me? I'm taking a holiday from the retail trade (from the Old French *retaillier*, to cut into small pieces, would you believe? I would hope from the selling of cloth or cheese or camel skins, rather than books) and giving Her Majesty's Government, bless its little woolly hat, a hand to sort out its problems. I happen to be aboard a warship of one of Her Majesty's allies, but that is what allies are for, is it not? Quite simple, really. It's not as if I had just crashed head-first into the sea in a plane with only one wing. That, I should think, requires a bit more explanation. Or don't you agree?"

Everything came flooding back: the plane coming to bits, bailing out, the crash... "Where's Chris?" she asked urgently. "Is he all right?"

"Chris? I take it you are referring to the other parachute freak. Why you couldn't have practised crashing planes and bailing out of them somewhere nearer home, I've no idea."

"Is he okay?" repeated Aisling.

"Fine, I should say. Probably enjoying beetroot soup and vodka at this very moment."

"Sorry?"

"He was picked up by the Russians, lucky man."

"The *Russians*?" Aisling sat up quickly. For a moment the cabin she was in circled around her and then it settled down again. She looked at John Smith in horror. "Have Shavitov and Lerntowski got out of prison, then? How on earth did they get here?"

He smiled. "A couple of enterprising gentlemen, our Shavitov and Lerntowski. A credit to S.K.U.N.K. But as far as I know, they're still behind bars. And anyway, what makes you think they're Russian?"

"Aren't they?"

"Not necessarily. No doubt they spent their innocent baby years somewhere in central Europe, but I don't see why you should blame poor Russia for them. She gets blamed for enough already."

"But you said Chris was picked up by the Russians."

"Isn't it marvellous to talk to someone who pays attention! The Russians I was referring to, however, are over there." John Smith waved a plump hand towards the cabin porthole. "This is a combined exercise by the Americans and Russians (or, to be more precise, and I'm sure Seamus would like us always to be precise, the United States' and Soviet forces). A marvellous example of *glasnost* and *perestroika*, that."

"Don't tell me," Aisling interrupted quickly before he could give her a lecture on the Russian language. "Openness and recon— struction. Do you really think Shavitov and Lerntowski are still in prison?"

"I haven't heard that they're not."

Aisling breathed a sigh of relief.

"I said I hadn't heard—I didn't say I knew that pair of lovable loonies was still safely locked up. They certainly haven't put their own personalised signatures on the charming little blackmail notes which have been circulating of late—I suppose S.K.U.N.K. could well be being run by someone else in the meantime."

"It's definitely S.K.U.N.K, though, is it?" Aisling shivered.

"Indubitably. From the Latin *in* meaning *not* and *dubium* meaning *doubt*. Or, as our American cousins would say, it sure is, sister."

"Oh."

"Now, if you're feeling strong enough, the captain would like to ask you a few questions. And so would I, for that matter. The main one being: was there anyone else on that plane besides you and—what's his name?—Chris?"

"No. There was just the two of us."

"Thank goodness for that. When they fished you out of the sea, I half feared that ghastly orange cat, or even dear old Seamus, might have been with you. At least they had the sense to stay at home. Now, come on and meet the American Navy."

There was a lot of the American Navy between the cabin and the bridge. And all of them seemed to find her very funny. Aisling, tripping along behind John Smith in a seaman's jumper about twenty sizes too big for her and with a pair of men's pyjama trousers rolled up round her bare ankles, didn't share the joke. She tried her best to look as if she walked through destroyers dressed like this every day of the week, but she was glad when they finally reached the bridge.

The captain, a tall, thin, middle-aged man with short grey hair and lots of gold braid about his uniform, shook her hand and asked her to sit down. No sooner had she done so, than he started firing questions at her: what were they doing here? where were they heading? who was the pilot? who had told them to come to this particular area of the North Sea? what did they hope to do when they reached their destination? what *was* their destination? who was giving them their orders? where had they come from?

He fixed her with cold blue eyes and Aisling suddenly remembered how she'd felt when she was eight and had been hauled before the headmistress for scribbling *Miss O'Keefe has false teefe* on the classroom blackboard. She looked to John Smith for help.

"Just tell the captain, Aisling. We have to

work together on this thing. If Seamus has found out something, we might as well share it."

Aisling sighed and told them all she knew. She ended with the compass going wrong and the plane falling to bits. "Do you think S.K.U.N.K. could have done something to make it break up like that?"

John Smith looked grave. "I don't know, Aisling, to be honest with you. There's certainly something funny going on just a few miles north of here. The same thing happened to the ships, didn't it sir?"

The captain nodded. "Sure. First the compass went, then the engine started to seize up and then every bit of metal on the ship began to show signs of fatigue. And the same for every ship in the fleet. If we hadn't turned back when we did, we'd have fallen apart."

"Just like your aeroplane. I wonder... Do you think they could have created a magnetic field, somehow?"

"Could be. But it'd have to be a darned powerful one."

"Hmm. An invisible magnetic barrier which would affect any ship or plane approaching Iceland. And nobody knowing how wide or how high it goes. Or how deep, for that matter.

Quite beautiful."

"What are you going to do about it?" Aisling asked.

John Smith shrugged. "Nothing, at the moment. We have to go back to Shetland and check every ship for structural damage. S.K.U.N.K. will be delighted."

"And then what? If you can't get near Iceland, how are you going to stop S.K.U.N.K. from blowing up the world or splitting it apart or whatever Seamus thinks they're doing?"

John Smith grinned at the captain. "I told you she was an intelligent girl. Put her finger on the nub of the problem immediately. There's something to be said for Irish education after all."

"Rats." Aisling glared at him. "I'm serious."

"And so, in my own inimitable way, am I. The short answer is: I don't know. We can try taking a submarine under the barrier or using a high-altitude plane to get over it, or we can take a convoy way out round the back to see if there's a gap there…"

"Or we could send in a nuclear warhead on a rocket," suggested the captain.

Aisling grinned. Then she realized he was serious. "You can't!" she protested.

The captain gave her a grim smile. "Why

not, kid? It's either them or us. If they really can interfere with the earth's crust, they can destroy the world. What's the destruction of one little island compared to that?"

"But..."

John Smith put a hand on her arm. "Don't worry, Aisling. Come on, you've had a hard day. I'm taking you below to get some rest."

"They wouldn't send a nuclear warhead to Iceland, would they?" Aisling asked as they went back to her cabin."

"They would if they thought it would do any good. Both sides would. Don't have any illusions about that."

"But what about all the people? And the birds and animals? Frankie was talking about seals and puffins and gerfalcons and things. They'd all be wiped out."

"*It's either them or us,*" quoted John Smith, mimicking the captain's accent. "No, I can see we'll have to do something about it. Somehow or other, we'll have to get there first, Aisling, before they go mad and start nuking everything."

"But how are we going to get past the...what did you call it?...magnetic wall?"

"I'll think of something. And be thankful that a rocket probably won't get past it either. Now, try to get some rest before we reach Lerwick."

7

Shavitov and Lerntowski Again

he short northern night was nearly over by the time they sighted the Shetland Islands, and the land was emerging as a dark, low shadow against the still colourless sky. Then the first streak of pink tinged the eastern horizon, seabirds appeared squawking round the ship, and finally the grey houses of Lerwick took substance, stretching down from the skyline until they reached out into the sea to welcome them.

The whole sound between Lerwick and the low island opposite was filled with warships. Aisling had never seen so many ships all together in one place. They had to thread their way between them in order to anchor near the harbour.

She was taken ashore with John Smith in

a motor dinghy. He pointed to a hotel to the left of the harbour. "We've set up headquarters there. I'll have to go along and make a report—are you coming?"

Aisling went with him along the narrow flagstoned street. It had no pavement—or maybe it was all pavement: the stones looked too uneven to be the surface of a street and the road itself seemed too narrow for traffic, although an army jeep, roaring up it and driving pedestrians into the shelter of doorways, proved that it was a road after all.

A soldier stood guard at the hotel entrance. John Smith showed him a pass, the soldier examined it, saluted and opened the door for them.

"Ash! Thank goodness you're all right!" Chris came bounding across the hotel lounge. His long hair looked as if it hadn't seen a comb since they'd left Dublin and he had a day's growth of dark stubble on his chin, but otherwise he looked fine. He took Aisling's arm and pushed her into a red plastic-covered sofa. He sat down opposite her. "You'll never guess what's happened!"

"You've found a way through the magnetic shield?"

Chris looked puzzled. "The what? Oh, that.

No, it's much more fantastic than that."

Aisling grinned. "Frankie's going to marry you?"

"Who? Oh, yes... Frankie." Chris's face fell. "Blast. I'd forgotten about her."

"That was quick."

"D'you think so?" He looked worried. Then his face cleared. "I'm sure she won't mind. After all, she's devoted to her work and I think I was more of a nuisance than anything else. Once she meets Olga..."

"Olga?"

"Didn't I tell you? I got picked up by this Russian ship and there was this fantastic second officer. Olga. You must meet her, Ash. You'll love her. She's fantastic!"

"So you said."

"Did I? She's small and dark and wears her hair in the most incredible bun and she's fantastically beautiful and she nursed me all last night. I don't know how I'd have pulled through without her."

Aisling looked at him in alarm. "Did you hurt yourself, then?"

Chris swept the hair back from his forehead to reveal a tiny piece of sticking plaster on his brow. "I could have bled to death. She was great, though. Healing hands, she has. Did I tell you that she speaks perfect English too?"

Aisling was relieved when John Smith interrupted them. He held out his hand. "You must be Chris, the dare-devil pilot. I'm delighted to make your acquaintance at last."

Chris jumped to his feet and an ashtray on the table hit the carpet. "This is John Smith," Aisling explained. "He works with the British Secret Service."

"Worked," John Smith corrected. "I'm just an adviser now. Which is why I'd like you to come with me and meet General Robson. There are some questions he'd like to ask you."

"What about me?" Aisling asked

"Why don't you have some breakfast and then go for a walk round the town. Broaden your mind, enlarge your horizons, embrace the challenge of new experiences. Unfortunately, I didn't bring an encyclopedia with me, but I'm sure the local library will be able to tell you all you need to know about the place. You can meet us back here at, let me see: say half past nine. I should have everything sorted out by then."

Aisling had had a cup of coffee on board the destroyer, but she was feeling quite hungry again. She ordered a large breakfast of fruit juice, grapefruit, coffee, bacon, sausages, rolls and toast and got great pleasure in telling the waitress that John Smith would pay the bill. Then she went out into the street again.

She decided to follow it out of town towards the coast. There might be a beach somewhere she could lie out on and she might even see some unusual wildlife: puffins or seals or something even more special: *Aisling Daly, schoolgirl ornithologist, discovers rare breed of seabird...*

She turned a corner by what looked like a large school and came to a point where the cliffs fell away to the sea. She sat down on the short springy grass between clumps of sea pinks and campions and looked around. Seabirds swooped over her head: herring gulls and black-headed gulls and straight-winged fulmars. Below her, the ledges were pied with sleek guillemots and piratical-looking razor bills and—she caught her breath—fat little birds with ludicrous expressions and rainbow beaks, which waddled up and down self-importantly on tiny ledges and then took off with a whirring flight, like overweight commuters with ulcers, on wings too small for their plump round bodies. Puffins!

Suddenly she remembered the time and looked at her watch. She'd just make it back to the hotel by half nine. As she got up, she noticed three people were walking towards her.

She glanced at them casually—and then looked again. She felt the skin crawling along her back and knew, suddenly, what it meant when people talked about their hair standing on end.

One of the three was a woman, small dark and pretty and wearing a strange uniform; but it was the other two who had made her skin crawl. One was big and bulky, the other small and thin, both wore dark suits and they looked exactly like Laurel and Hardy. But Aisling had met them before and knew that there was nothing funny about them. Their names were Shavitov and Lerntowski and they were the S.K.U.N.K. agents she had thought were safely locked up in jail!

For a minute, she was rooted to the spot. The trio had stopped too and were staring at her. Suddenly the big man, Shavitov, came towards her.

Aisling turned and ran. She heard his footsteps behind her. She ran faster, past the school and down into the town. She didn't dare look round, but she was sure he must be gaining on her. She remembered his incredible strength and the hatred he'd had for her the last time they'd met—which must be even greater now, she thought wretchedly, as she'd been largely responsible for putting him in prison.

She stumbled on one of the uneven paving stones in the middle of the street and nearly fell. He was right behind her—she could feel his presence. And, ahead of her, walking casually up the narrow street, was—she couldn't believe her eyes—the small owl-faced American who'd been spying on Seamus back in Dublin!

She looked desperately to either side, but the street was lined with houses with closed doors. If she stopped to knock on one, Shavitov and the other man would certainly catch her.

She made a quick decision. As she reached the owl-faced man, she tried to get round him as they'd been taught, for months on end it had seemed at the time, by Mrs Marshal in hockey, by pretending to be about to pass him on one side and then dodging at the last minute and slipping past him on the other. It worked!

She ran on, her side hurting, her breath coming in short gasps: she wouldn't be able to keep this up much longer. Why hadn't she bothered to take hockey training more seriously at school?

And then, from behind her, there came a shout. She looked over her shoulder. Shavitov was sprawled full-length on the uneven flagstones, Owl-face's umbrella was lying on the street beside him and Owl-face himself was bending over Shavitov, trying to help him up.

Not knowing what had happened but delighted that Shavitov had been stopped, Aisling found new energy and forced herself to continue running until she reached the hotel door.

The soldier on guard beside it was the most welcome person she had ever met. She was tempted to throw herself into his arms— especially as he was slim and dark and marvellously good-looking in his uniform. Instead, she smiled at him, panted "I'm with John Smith," pushed the door open and collapsed onto one of the red armchairs in the lounge.

John Smith and Chris had been waiting for her. Chris rushed over. "Are you all right, Ash? You're as white as a sheet."

John Smith looked her up and down and raised an eyebrow. "Keeping fit's all very well, Aisling, but you look as if you've been overdoing it. Personally, I never could understand what anyone sees in jogging—it wears out your shoes, for one thing, and must shake your brain into something resembling scrambled eggs. You should give it up, you know, and try yoga."

"Shavitov was after me!" Aisling gasped.

His smile vanished. "Shavitov? Are you sure?"

"Certain. Lerntowski was there too. And Owl-face."

"Who?"

"Owl-face. You know, the American with the glasses who was in your bookshop."

"Ah, him. The one who was interested in volcanoes."

"That's right. Shavitov must have crashed into him or something. Anyway, it slowed him down enough for me to get away."

"Good for Owl-face, then." John Smith seemed amused.

"It's not funny. He's one of the enemy and everywhere we go he seems to be one step ahead of us. How does he always know where to find us next?"

John Smith shrugged. "Talent?"

Chris finally managed to get a word in. "What are you two talking about?" he asked impatiently. "Who's Shavitwhatever? What happened?"

"Shavitov is the strong-arm man of a very nasty gentleman called Lerntowski. You're lucky you've never had occasion to make their acquaintance, Christopher, my lad. Mind you," John Smith looked thoughtful, "are you sure it was them? They ought to be in prison."

"It was them," said Aisling with a shudder. "They were talking to a woman up on the cliffs—a small dark woman with black hair done up in a bun and a queer sort of uniform."

John Smith looked at Chris. He smiled. "Small and dark and wearing her hair in a bun. And in uniform. It couldn't have been your Olga, could it?"

"Was she pretty?" Chris asked Aisling.

"Well, yes. I suppose so. Though I didn't have time to look at her properly. As soon as I saw it was Shavitov and Lerntowski she was with, I ran."

"Hmm. Curiouser and curiouser, as the White Knight said. Or was it Alice?"

Aisling sighed in exasperation. "Don't show off. And why is it curious, anyway? If S.K.U.N.K. can make earthquakes and volcanoes happen all over the world, they can surely get a couple of their people out of jail."

She looked anxiously towards the hotel door. "I'll bet they're waiting out there now. I'm certainly not going out on my own again."

"No. You're both going out together. In fact, your pumpkin has arrived." John Smith returned the wave of an American soldier who had just come in through the door. "Come on, Cinderella. And you too Buttons. I've managed to arrange for a plane to take both of you back to Dublin. It's handy having a bit of influence now and again."

"Aren't you coming?" Aisling asked.

"No. I've work to do here. Apart from which," he winked at her, "someone has to keep an eye on our bomb-happy friends. I'll feel easier when I know you're out of here, especially with Shavitov and Lerntowski around. And try to persuade Seamus to keep out of this too: he's far too old to be playing spies."

Aisling grinned. "You try telling him that."

"I'm serious. This could get very nasty. Do your best anyway." He stood up. "Are you ready? I'll just check that the coast is clear."

He opened the hotel door cautiously and peered up and down the street. When he came inside again, he was grinning like a mischievous schoolboy. "Shavitov's in a doorway opposite, looking like a grizzly bear pretending to be invisible. I can't see the others, but they're probably around somewhere. The jeep's just outside and the driver's ready. Now, run for it!"

He held the door open and Aisling and Chris raced for the jeep. Aisling looked back as they rattled down the uneven street. Shavitov had come out of the doorway and was standing in the middle of the road, a large squat ominous figure, staring after them. "I wonder where the others are?" she whispered.

They soon found out!

8
Car Chase

s they turned left at the harbour to take the road leading south to Sumburgh Airport, a sleek black car appeared behind them. Aisling glanced back.

"It's them!" she said in horror. "Shavitov and Lerntowski! They're going to catch us!"

Chris turned to their driver, a freckled-faced American sergeant with short fair hair cut in a neat crewcut. "Do you think you can lose that car behind us?"

"Sure thing." The sergeant grinned. He pressed his foot on the accelerator and the jeep leapt forwards. Aisling looked behind anxiously: the black car was still there.

The jeep turned sharply to the right and drove through a maze of side streets. "I think we've lost them!" Aisling shouted.

The driver turned, winked at her and raised a hand with the thumbs-up sign.

But as they left Lerwick behind them and started on the long narrow road which wound southwards between low treeless hills and the sea, the black car appeared behind them again.

The sergeant was enjoying himself. He forced the jeep to its limits, screeching round corners so that Aisling and Chris had to hang on to the sides of their seats to avoid being thrown to the floor. Aisling was reminded of the time she was chased by S.K.U.N.K. in Switzerland— she'd survived Tante Margarethe's driving then, she thought; she might just possibly survive this.

Fortunately, the road was quiet. Whenever their driver caught up with a car going in their direction, he blared his horn and swung past it, practically forcing it off the road and leaving its driver, white-faced and swearing, to the mercies of the black car behind—which roared past with equal recklessness.

It came so close sometimes that Aisling could see the evil pudgy face of Shavitov behind the wheel and the thin, pale, ascetic features of Lerntowski beside him. She held on to her seat and concentrated on looking ahead, trying to pretend they weren't there.

"Don't worry, Ash!" Chris shouted above the noise of the wind rushing past their ears. "They can't overtake us—the road's too narrow."

And he was right. Their driver refused to give way and stayed on the crown of the road, swerving to his own side only when a car came towards them. And then only at the last minute. Each time Aisling was sure that this was it—they would certainly crash this time. She imagined the headlines in the paper: *Irish schoolgirl and young Irish pilot killed in crashed American army jeep in Shetland!* Whatever would her parents think?

Each time, however, they escaped by a hair's breadth and miraculously no innocent traffic was harmed. The sheep which grazed beside the unfenced road were in even more danger: Aisling visualized one crashing into the front of the jeep and its bloody carcase being splattered all over the road. She shut her eyes and shuddered. She was extremely relieved when Sumburgh Airport appeared ahead.

A plane bearing the insignia of the US Air Force was waiting on the runway. Skirting the main airport building, the sergeant drove straight for it. The black car followed.

In the building a siren went off, causing a

flock of seagulls at the side of the runway to rise into the air, wheeling and squawking like a blizzard of raucous snowflakes. A police car followed by a fire engine moved out towards them.

The jeep skidded to a halt beside the plane. A man in airforce uniform poked his head out of the cockpit. "What the...?"

"Emergency, Mac," shouted the sergeant. "Get these folk out of here!"

"Out you go!" He pushed Chris and Aisling out of the jeep. "Hurry up! Move!"

Chris pulled her up the steps into the plane. She stopped at the door and looked back. The jeep had turned and was racing towards the black car. She watched as the two vehicles headed straight for one another. They *had* to crash!

She shut her eyes.

There was a loud bang.

She opened them again.

The jeep must have swerved at the very last moment. It had hit the car side-on—it skidded like a curling stone on ice along the concrete runway, sparks flying out from beneath it. The jeep turned with a squeal of brakes and followed it.

"Come on, Ash!" Chris pulled her into the

plane.

The pilot was staring down the runway where the jeep, the fire engine and the police car were converging on the suddenly motionless black car. "Jeez!" he exclaimed. "Well I'll be dog-blasted! What in the heck's going on?"

"We're the passengers you were waiting for," yelled Chris. "You're to take us to Dublin. Can we leave now?"

The pilot took another look at the chaos behind them on the runway. "I see your point, bud. It might be a good idea."

As the plane rose into the air, Aisling looked back. The black car had recovered and was speeding towards the Lerwick road; the other vehicles were trying to head it off...

And then the plane banked and they all disappeared from sight under the wing. And after that, all she could see was the waves beneath them. She felt cold: had Shavitov and Lerntowski escaped again?

9
Council of War

oo old! That young man has an inflated opinion of himself. I may be a cripple, but I'm not senile yet. I'll show him!" Chris had given Seamus John Smith's advice to keep out of things and now Seamus looked as if he was about to have a fit. Mulligan, who had slunk into the studio on the heels of Aisling and Chris, took refuge under the bed.

Aisling smothered a grin. "How?" she asked innocently.

"How? By getting to Iceland before them and dealing with S.K.U.N.K. myself."

"But nobody can get to Iceland—S.K.U.N.K. have got some sort of magnetic shield all round it. We told you. Any plane or boat trying to get anywhere near just falls apart."

"So? Whatever man has made, man can get

round. O'Toole's law. It just needs a bit of thought."

Seamus doodled on the pad in front of him. Magnets appeared, long nails, islands and volcanoes, boats...

"That's it!" he said suddenly. "The obvious answer. Now, where is he? I was reading something about him just the other day."

"Who?" asked Chris.

"Thorwald." Seamus rubbed his chin with the piece of charcoal he'd been sketching with. It broke, leaving a grey smudge on his face, and a piece fell onto the floor. Mulligan arched a paw round it from under the bed, pulled it towards him, chewed it and spat it out with a disgusted expression. Tiny pieces of wet charcoal sprayed over Aisling's runners. She kicked at him. He glared back at her with an expression of aggrieved innocence and jumped up on to the bed, where he started to wash himself noisily.

She looked back at Seamus. "Thorwald who?"

"Thorwaldson."

"*Who?*"

"Who? Who? You sound like an owl. Be quiet and let me think. Trying to remember anything with you hooting at me is impossible. Did either of you read anything recently about a

Viking ship? No, of course you didn't. You never read anything useful."

"As it happens," Chris said smugly, "I did. I take it you're referring to the good ship *Fafnir*, at present sailing from Bergen to the Isle of Man, retracing the Viking trade routes? I read an article about it in the *Shetland Times* this morning while we were waiting for Aisling. They rather go in for Vikings in Shetland."

"Do they now? You surprise me," grunted Seamus, not sounding in the least surprised. "But that's the ship all right. I want you to go to Douglas right away, Christopher, and tell Thorwald I need to borrow his ship. If he hurries, he might make it here by tomorrow."

"Who's Douglas?" Aisling asked.

Seamus raised his eyes to the ceiling. "Who's Douglas, she asks! God help your geography teacher! He's a dog in the *Magic Roundabout*."

"The what?"

Chris grinned. "Sorry, Seamus. That was Dougal." He winked at Aisling. "We can all make mistakes. Douglas, to keep you straight, Aisling, is the capital of the Isle of Man."

"Hmph," said Seamus.

Aisling sighed. She decided to try again. "Talking of people..." she started.

"Which we weren't," Seamus pointed out.

"How did Shavitov and Lerntowski get to Shetland? I thought they were in prison."

"Ah yes. I checked up on them yesterday. I had thought that at least Swiss jails could be depended on, but it would appear otherwise: our fat friend and his master escaped a few months ago and nobody bothered to tell us. Just before all the earthquakes started, in fact. Which is all the more reason to believe that S.K.U.N.K.'s behind all this. Now, get a move on. You should be half-way to the Isle of Man by now, Christopher, not sitting around here wasting my time."

"You don't even know the *Fafnir*'s reached Douglas yet," objected Chris. "And what makes you think that Thorwald, or whatever he's called, will up anchor and come running just because you say so?"

Seamus grunted. "Not everyone treats me with the same lack of respect as yourself. But more to the point, when he knows what's up, he'll come. Hold on a minute while I write a note.

"There. I've asked him to meet us at Carlingford tomorrow afternoon. He should feel at home in a Viking port and it'll be less public than Dun Laoghaire or Dublin. If you fly over there right away, you should be back here by this evening. In the meantime, I'll get everything organized this end."

"Okay," said Chris. "If you say so. But I'll have to check if there's a flight. And I need money for the ticket. You seem to forget that, thanks to your last bright idea, my own plane's sunk without trace in the middle of the North Atlantic."

"Stop moaning, boy—I presume you had it insured. And as for the rest, ask Florence. Now hurry—we've wasted too much time already."

"Can you ring Mum and say I'm staying another night?" Aisling asked.

"No."

"Why? She won't mind."

"Because you're not."

"Not what?"

"Not staying another night. Nor are you pretending to stay another night and gadding off to the Isle of Man with Christopher here. You were supposed to keep his mind on his work when I sent you up to Shetland with him—what happened there wasn't much of a job reference. This time, I'd prefer it if you stayed at home. Or went back to school for a change to try to improve your mind."

"I thought you thought school was a waste of time," Aisling pointed out. "And anyway, it's the holidays. It's been the holidays for the past month. There's nothing stopping me from helping you again."

"Yes there is: me. Now get out and leave me in peace."

"But that's not fair! You've got to let me help."

"Life is unfair, as you have no doubt been told before." Seamus picked up his sketch pad. "Goodbye."

Chris stood up. "Come on, Ash. Before he gets a heart attack. You know people of his age shouldn't get too excited. 'Bye, Seamus. Look after yourself."

He pulled Aisling through the door just before a heavy book which had been lying on the bedside table hit the other side of it with a resounding thud.

"Temper!" murmured Chris.

"Rats!" said Aisling feelingly.

She cycled home deep in thought. Seamus was an opinionated, bloody-minded, stubborn old man, but he was not keeping her out of this adventure. She didn't mind all that much, she admitted to herself, not going on another aeroplane so soon after the crash—she shook her head to dislodge the picture, which had suddenly appeared in her mind, of Chris's plane hitting the water. But she certainly wasn't going to sit at home while Seamus and Florence and Chris (and Thorwald, whoever he was) set out to save the world. It was just a matter of making a plan. Seamus had told Chris to ask Thorwald to be at Carlingford with his ship the next afternoon...

As soon as she got home, she phoned CIE Then: "Mum. Can I go to Carlingford for a few days?"

"Carlingford? Why?"

"Well, you know Catherine Ruttledge? Her family have a cottage up there for the summer. That was them on the phone just now—they've invited me to stay with them. To keep Catherine company."

"I didn't think you and Catherine were such close friends."

"Well...we're not, really. Only everyone's away at the moment. And we get on all right. Can I go?"

"I suppose so. If you're sure they want you."

"Great. I'll get the morning train tomorrow and they'll meet me at Dundalk. I'll just go and pack."

That night, another thought struck her. She set her alarm to wake early and cycled up to

Seamus's house in Dalkey. She went round to the back door.

It was open. The kitchen looked as if a bomb had hit it. Cardboard boxes full of tins and packets, sacks of vegetables and crates of fruit covered every available surface. The table was like a cake stall in a church sale. Aisling grinned. Having once, long ago, practically died of starvation, Florence made sure she would never run short of food again.

Florence looked up as Aisling came in. "If you've come to see Seamus, I suggest you go home again. He's in no mood for visitors."

A blast from the whistle on the speaking tube to the studio proved how right she was. She sighed, wiped her hands on her pinny and picked up the tube. "Yes?"

"Where the blazes are my purple socks?"

"In the drawer at the side of your bed with the rest of your socks. Where they always are."

"They're not."

"Look again." Aisling was amazed at the way Florence kept her temper.

"Hmph."

The speaking tube clicked and was silent.

"I don't know how you stand it," she said.

"'You're young,'" Florence said, as if that were an answer.

"Did Seamus say when you're leaving?"

"As soon as Christopher returns."

"I thought he was coming back last night?"

Florence carefully lined a pie dish with pastry. "I gather there wasn't a plane."

"Oh." Aisling looked round. "Where's Mulligan?"

Florence gestured with her head towards a cupboard by the window. "Keeping a low profile, as I believe you young ones say nowadays."

At first Aisling couldn't see him. Then she realized that there was an object on top of the cupboard, squeezed between it and the ceiling. When she looked closely, she could see that it was Mulligan: his eyes were narrowed to yellow slits, his ears were flat and his tail, which hung down at the far side of the cupboard, was lashing violently from side to side. He reminded her of a tiger treed by a pack of dogs.

"What on earth's he doing up there?"

"I stood on him." Florence didn't sound very sympathetic.

"Poor Mulligan. What are you going to do with him when you leave? Are you taking him with you?"

"No. Seamus insists we leave him behind. Mrs Byrne will look after him."

"I'll take him outside—he looks miserable here. Come on, Mulligan. Down you come!"

The cat gave Florence a filthy look and moved further back into the corner.

"You must have done more than just stand on him. Can I borrow a piece of cheese or something from the fridge?"

"Take what you like, child, only get out of here. And take that orange monster with you. It was bad enough trying to work with him putting his nose into everything, but the two of you together are impossible."

"Sorry. I'll get him down in a minute." Aisling took a corner of Brie from the fridge, waved it in front of Mulligan and backed through the piles of boxes to the door. "Come on, Mulligan. Food!"

Mulligan nose twitched. He clawed his way to the front of the cupboard and then launched himself. The cupboard rocked and plates crashed ominously inside it. He landed on the table between a sponge cake and a plate of scones. Without pausing, he turned and leapt for the floor. His hind legs hit the sponge cake, sending it flying.

Aisling picked him up, stuffed the cheese into his open mouth and slung him over her shoulder. "'Bye," she said hurriedly. "Have a good journey."

She shut the door before Florence could answer.

She'd brought a large canvas bag with her. She knelt down, opened the zip and stuffed Mulligan inside. Fortunately he was a cat who liked travelling in bags. She closed the zip, humped the bag onto the back carrier of her bike and started off. *Schoolgirl caught kidnapping cat!* she thought. But if she was going off on her own, she needed someone to keep her company. And if Shavitov turned up again, she'd have a weapon: he was extremely allergic to cats.

10
Carlingford

he rest of her plan worked equally well. She had already packed her clothes into a rucksack and all she needed to do now was to put some cold meat and biscuits into her pockets, in case Mulligan got hungry: with any luck he'd sleep most of the way, but it was as well to be prepared.

She took the DART to Connolly Station and changed to the Belfast train. She found a window seat, put her rucksack into the rack and settled the bag with Mulligan between her legs under the table. It twitched once and then was quiet.

Mulligan stayed quiet until the trolley with tea and sandwiches came round. The smell of the sandwiches, even through their polythene wrapping, must have penetrated the canvas bag. It twitched between her feet. She grinned and slid back the zip a couple of inches. An orange paw appeared at the opening. She glanced up in alarm, but no-one in the carriage was watching her. Hastily, she slipped a piece of meat from her pocket into the bag. The paw disappeared. She pushed some more meat and a couple of biscuits in and did up the zip. The bag squirmed as Mulligan twisted round to get at the food.

"Are you all right, girl?"

Aisling jumped.

An elderly nun sitting opposite was peering anxiously across the table at her.

Aisling forced a smile and tried to squash Mulligan down in the bag with her feet. "I'm fine, thanks, Sister. I was just...thinking."

"You'd be better now with that bag out of the way. I'm sure the gentleman here will put it up in the rack for you."

A large weather-beaten man who looked like a farmer and who was sitting next to the nun looked up, embarrassed. "Of course, Sister." He stood up clumsily and stretched out his hand.

"No!" Aisling realized she sounded too extreme. "It's all right. I'm okay, really I am."

She was delighted when a voice from the

corridor interrupted them: "Excuse me, ma'am. Would you say that that seat opposite you was in an on-going occupied situation?"

The nun looked dazed.

Aisling's delight turned to horror. The American raising his felt hat and smiling politely down at the nun through dark-framed glasses was none other than Owl-face! Where on earth had he come from? She'd left him in Shetland!

"The seat's taken," she said quickly.

"Do sit down," said the nun at the same time. She frowned at Aisling. "That seat is free, as you know," she reminded her.

Aisling felt herself blushing.

Owl-face sat down. "Thank you kindly, folks." He beamed round the compartment. "It sure is a lovely day weatherwise, wouldn't you say?"

The nun smiled. The farmer nodded glumly. "Too fine," he muttered. "Another few weeks of this and we'll be ruined, so we will."

Owl-face turned to Aisling. "It is Aisling, isn't it? I was hoping to interface with you. How is my old buddy, John Smith?"

Aisling stared out of the window, her back to him.

"Well now, girl. Is that anyway to behave?

And the gentleman asking you a civil question."

Aisling wished the nun back in County Clare, or wherever it was she came from. She forced a smile. "Mammy told me not to speak to strange men, Sister."

"Holy Mary Mother of God! The manners of the young folk nowadays! *Me mammy told me not to speak to strange men*! Whatever will the gentleman think of you? And he a friend of a friend of yours! And a visitor too! What part of America do you come from, so?"

"San Francisco, Sister." Owl-face beamed at her again. The nun simpered.

Owl-face turned back to Aisling. "So you're travelling at this moment in time to Belfast, are you, Aisling? Is your godfather relocating himself too?"

The nun looked at her severely, waiting for her to answer.

Again Aisling tried to smile. "I'm afraid you've made a mistake," she said firmly. "You must be thinking of someone else. My name's Mary and I don't know anyone called John Smith."

"Uhuh. Is that a fact? Well now, allow me to apologize. I figured, if you had been Aisling, you might have been headed for a crisis-situation situation and would have appreciated some help, assistance-wise."

"Well I'm not and I don't."

The nun pursed her lips at this rudeness. Aisling ignored her. She dragged her rucksack down from the rack, slung it over her shoulder and picked up the bag with Mulligan in it. "Excuse me."

Owl-face stood up to let her pass. He looked at her thoughtfully. "Uhuh. That bag looks kind of heavy to me. Let me share with you in carrying it." He put out a hand.

Aisling snatched the bag away from him. "I'm fine. Thanks very much."

She didn't look round until she was safely in the next carriage. To her relief, he hadn't followed her. Maybe he had believed he'd made a mistake: after all, he must be very short-sighted to wear those awful glasses. She went on up the train, thinking that the further she got from him the better. The bag was unwieldy, her rucksack kept slipping and knocking into people and she got tired of continually apologising—but at least Mulligan stayed quiet. She found an empty seat near the front of the train and waited for Dundalk.

Dundalk station was quiet. Aisling felt terribly exposed as she crossed the platform. If Owl-face saw her now...

She got out of the station as quickly as possible and stopped to put down the canvas bag: Mulligan weighed a ton. To her horror, a thin well-manicured hand attached itself to the handle of the bag.

"Well, well. Isn't life just one big coincidence?" Owl-face picked up the bag. "Goll-y. It sure is heavy, weight-wise. What have you got in there? Solid gold bars?"

Mulligan woke and stretched himself. The bag wobbled in Owl-face's hand. Bumps appeared and disappeared in the canvas.

"Well now. Isn't that interesting!" Owl-face started to open the zip.

"Hey! Give me that back! It's my bag!" Aisling grabbed the bag from him. Owl-face held on. Three long white whiskers and a yellow eye appeared at the opening he'd made.

A passing couple looked at them curiously.

"Help!" shouted Aisling. "He's trying to steal my bag!"

The woman hesitated. She glanced at her husband. He took her arm and hurried her on.

Owl-face raised his hat. "Sorry, kid. I was just trying to help, assistance-wise."

He stood back to let her pass.

"You go first," said Aisling.

"Negative. In the context of male-female interrelationships, ladies have the advantage. Have a nice day."

The couple had stopped further along the pavement and were looking back curiously. There was nothing for it. Aisling picked up the bag again and walked on.

Now what? She had to get rid of him somehow before she got on the Carlingford bus.

She looked round, expecting to see him behind her. He had disappeared. Not quite believing her luck, she stopped the first passerby and asked the way to the bus station.

It seemed miles away. She dragged Mulligan past a huge building (Harp Brewery, a sign said) and along a deserted street: Owl-face could murder her here, she thought, and no one would see. She looked round anxiously and hurried on, her rucksack becoming more and more heavy and the bag with Mulligan weighing her down. She came to a sort of square where there were, at least, more people about, but there was still no sign of a bus station. She transferred the bag to her other hand, asked again, and was directed down a shabby tree-lined road with deserted buildings on either side. She couldn't help looking round every few minutes: still no one behind her. She told herself that he could be dodging behind one of the trees every time she turned round— but surely she'd have seen him? He must have given up, she thought with relief.

The Carlingford bus was already waiting when she finally reached the bus station. The driver started the engine. Aisling climbed on board and sat down near the back, clutching the bag with Mulligan tightly on her lap. She'd made it!

And then the driver opened the doors again. A small thin man with a soft hat and owlish glasses climbed in, panting. He raised his hat to the driver. "Thanks, bud."

Aisling shrank back in her seat, trying to hide behind the woman in front, but it was no use. He'd seen her. He'd probably seen her all the time, she told herself bitterly. *Schoolgirl outwits foreign spy!* Rats.

He sat down in the seat beside her. "Hi," he said. "We seem to be in a recurrent-meeting situation. How about being friends, relation-wise?"

"Why are you following me?" Aisling hissed angrily.

"Me? Following you? If I may say so, you seem to have a problem, kid."

"*I* seem to have a problem?" Aisling turned her back on him and stared out of the window.

"Uhuh. So now you're mad with me. Just because I happen to be going the same direction as yourself, destinationwise." He paused for a moment. "Where are we going, then?" he added.

"There you are. You *are* following me!"

Owl-face smiled. "Only for your own good, kid. You'd be prudent to trust me."

"Huh."

"Don't I present as trustworthy?" He grinned at her. "Little old ladies ask me continually to see them across the road. Kids offer me a lick of their lollipops. Even dogs—that's not a dog you have in there, is it?—think I'm the cat's pyjamas."

"Too bad on them."

"Percentagewise, you've got to admit I'm a nice guy. All the evidence points towards it."

Aisling didn't believe him. "If you want to know where I'm going, I'm going to stay with my friend Catherine in Carlingford. So tell that to S.K.U.N.K. and let them do what they want with it."

"Uhuh." Owl-face sounded thoughtful. "You figure I'm associated with S.K.U.N.K., situationwise?"

Aisling didn't bother to reply.

Owl-face sighed. "I'm not, you know." He placed two fingers on his heart. "Scouts honour. I'm a nice guy. I'm in a positive-interaction situation with your friend John Smith and he sent me here to find out from you what Seamus is up to. And that's the whole ball game, honest."

"Well isn't that just too bad. What a waste of a journey for you. You'll have to tell John Smith, if you know him, that Seamus is back in Dublin. The last time I saw him he told me to go away and stop annoying him. So I did."

"Uhuh. That sounds affirmative, prob-abilitywise." Owl-face lay back in his seat and tipped his hat over his eyes. Aisling hoped he'd go to sleep. But he spoke again.

"Seems to me, you aren't too fond of your godfather, emotionwise."

"I hate him." That was the truth, she thought bitterly. "He never tells you anything and just uses you when it suits him and then tells you to go away like a good little girl when things begin to get exciting."

"Uhuh. And are things beginning to get exciting?"

Aisling bit her tongue. Why hadn't she kept her mouth shut? "Everyone knows something's going on," she said quickly. "It's in all the papers."

"Uhuh." He was silent for a long time, leaning back in his seat with his eyes closed. Then he sat up and looked at her. "Well, it was a pleasure entering into a meaningful dialogue with you, Aisling. Here's my card, just in case you should think of anything else to tell me. It's my Dublin address."

Aisling took the card and put it, without looking at it, in her pocket. She'd fooled him! The only danger now was if Thorwald's boat— what was it called? the *Fafnir*—had already arrived in Carlingford.

But there was no Viking ship in Carlingford harbour when they arrived. Aisling breathed a sigh of relief. She said goodbye to Owl-face as the bus stopped on the sea front. "I take it you'll be going straight back to Dublin. Sorry you've had a wasted trip."

He smiled at her. Then he looked round at the hill behind the town, the little harbour flanked by its ruined castle and the Mountains of Mourne across the lough. "Well, I don't know," he said slowly. "I think I might just take myself a short vacation, holidaywise. I wonder if a guy can hire a sailing boat here."

"I'm sure you can't" said Aisling quickly. "They're all private. And shouldn't you be going back to Dublin to keep an eye on Seamus?"

"Uhuh." Owl-face smiled down at her again. "I figure Seamus can look after himself. I guess I'll stay on here for a bit, timewise, and see your beautiful countryside."

Blast, thought Aisling. Now she really would have to go and see Catherine. She shouldered her rucksack, turned her back on the sea and hauled Mulligan, still in his bag, up a narrow street to the Ruttledge's holiday house.

Mrs Ruttledge came to the door. She looked surprised. "Aisling! How... nice to see you." Her gaze went from the rucksack to the bag at Aisling's feet and stopped at the large ginger cat draped over her shoulder. Mulligan had had enough of being stuck in a bag and had insisted on coming out. Her face fell. "Catherine didn't say anything..."

"It's all right, Mrs Ruttledge. "I'm meeting my godfather on his boat. Only it's not arrived yet so I thought I'd look Catherine up instead."

"Oh." The relief on Mrs Ruttledge's face was obvious. "Well, in that case... You'd better come in and wait here. Is that cat yours?"

"Well, sort of."

Mulligan realized he was being spoken about. He slithered down Aisling's front and twined himself, purring louder than a bus engine, around Mrs Ruttledge's legs. He looked up at her and miaowed plaintively.

"Oh, the poor darling. He must be hungry."

"Probably," said Aisling without much sympathy. "He always is. But I did feed him on the train.

Mulligan miaowed again, heartbreakingly. Mrs Ruttledge fell for it. "Come on, pussy. I'll get you something to eat." He raced into the kitchen after her and skidded to a halt in front of the fridge. He even had the tact to wrap himself around her legs one last time before throwing himself on the saucer of food she put down for him. Aisling grinned.

"You can wait in the front room," Mrs Ruttledge suggested. "Catherine's out sailing— she shouldn't be long."

"Thanks, Mrs Ruttledge."

The window had a superb view down to the harbour. A couple of kids were messing in a dinghy, an old man was fishing from the jetty and an elegant young woman in skin-tight pink jeans and a shocking-pink sweater was sitting on the castle steps talking to... It was Owl-face again! Why didn't he go away? She began to wonder if he'd believed her after all: from where he was standing, he could see both the house she was in and the harbour. Was he still spying on her?

She moved back from the window, picked the morning paper up from the coffee table and tried to read. There had been another bad earthquake in America and earth tremors right across Europe. Obviously the American and Russian navies—and John Smith—hadn't yet managed to stop S.K.U.N.K. If nobody stopped them soon, the whole world looked as if it would be torn apart. She shivered. She didn't want to die yet.

She felt better when Mulligan, sleek and contented after a huge plate of fresh mackerel, nudged the door open and came and joined her. He jumped onto her lap, pushed his mackerel-smelling nose into her face, licked her chin, turned round a couple of times and finally settled himself across her knees. She was glad she'd brought him with her. With S.K.U.N.K. shaking the world to bits, Owl-face down at the harbour and no sign of Chris or Seamus, it was nice to have one friend at least.

Suddenly she heard a shout from the harbour. She jumped up. Mulligan slid off her lap onto the floor and glared at her accusingly. She ignored him. Outside, everyone was pointing excitedly towards the sea.

And there, on the horizon, was a large square red and white striped sail.

The *Fafnir* was coming!

11
The *Fafnir*

he watched from the cottage as the Viking ship passed Greenore point. Soon she could see it plainly, its red and white sail billowing in the breeze and its fierce dragon head cleaving the waves.

Then a large removals van crossed in front of the harbour, momentarily obstructing her view. It stopped at the foot of the castle. To Aisling's surprise, Chris got down from the cab: Seamus and Florence must be in the removals van! She had to warn them that Owl-face was waiting for them!

"I've just seen my godfather," she shouted through to Mrs Ruttledge. "Thanks for letting me wait here. Goodbye!" She picked up her rucksack and Mulligan and rushed out of the house.

Too late!

Owl-face was already there, deep in conversation with Chris. And beside them was the elegant young woman in pink. Aisling noticed with a sinking feeling that her shiny black hair was drawn back in a bun.

"Aisling!" Chris was grinning like one of those idiots in an advert for sweat-removing washing powder. "Guess what? You'll never believe this, but Olga's here!"

Fortunately, before Aisling had a chance to reply, Florence came out of the van. She didn't look pleased. "How on earth did you get here, Aisling? And what is Mulligan doing with you? We were looking for him everywhere this morning."

"Sorry." Aisling felt herself blushing. "I didn't mean to worry you. But Seamus wouldn't let me come with you and I had to get here alone and I just wanted Mulligan for company..." She heard herself sounding more and more pathetic.

"I expected more consideration from you. And what about your parents? I suppose you never thought of them either?"

"I did. I told them I'd been invited to spend a week or so with a friend in Carlingford."

"That was very naughty of you, child."

Aisling bit her lip. "Please, Florence. Can't I stay? I won't be any trouble and I may be able to help."

"Well..." Florence hesitated. "I must admit that, if it were up to me, I'd put you on the first bus home. Quite apart from all the trouble you've caused and the fact that you've deceived your parents, I wasn't at all happy about the way we looked after you last time. But I suppose I'd better let Seamus decide what to do with you. In you go, now, and see what he says—I have some last-minute shopping to do."

"Thanks."

Quickly, before Florence could change her mind, Aisling opened the door to the back of the removals van.

Seamus, wearing a multicoloured woollen cap and a matching sweater, was sitting up in his huge brass bed surrounded by all the boxes and crates Florence had brought with them. He was drawing, as usual, on a pad on his lap.

"About time too," he grumbled. "You'd think I was just another of your blasted blankets or a tin of baked beans, the way you leave me in here." He looked up, saw who it was, and scowled. "And just what d'you think you are doing here?"

"We've got to *do* something!" Aisling said urgently.

He looked at her drily. "No doubt. Otherwise we'd all seize up. But why the sudden interest in action? And, to repeat my question, what are you—not to mention that orange scavenger—doing here? I thought we'd left you in Dalkey."

Aisling glanced at Mulligan who was nosing about amongst the boxes, looking for something to eat. She turned back to Seamus. "The *Fafnir*'s coming in and Chris is out there talking to two S.K.U.N.K. agents! We've got to get rid of them before it arrives!"

"You still haven't answered my question."

"Not now!" Aisling could have strangled him. "I told you, the *Fafnir* will be here at any minute. What are we going to do?"

Seamus took her seriously at last. "Which two agents?"

"That Olga woman who was talking to Shavitov and Lerntowski in Lerwick, and the American with the glasses who was spying on us in Dublin. And Chris is so besotted with the Russian woman, he doesn't care."

"Hmm. So you think they're both S.K.U.N.K. agents, do you?"

"Oh, be your age!" Aisling bit her tongue.

"Of course, they're from S.K.U.N.K. Who else could they be?"

Seamus grinned infuriatingly. "I am my age. Which is why I don't jump to conclusions like some young people I know who ought to keep a civil tongue in their heads. That Olga woman, as you call her, is an officer in the Russian Navy—or so Christopher tells me. The Russians are as worried about S.K.U.N.K. as we are. Ergo, she is quite possibly fighting for Civilisation (whatever that may mean, and I suspect it means precious little) like the rest of us."

"But she was talking to Shavitov and Lerntowski in Lerwick. I saw her."

"You saw someone who looked like her. And, even if it had been her, talking to that glorious pair of criminals isn't in itself a crime. As for your other spy, we know nothing at all about him. Who does he say he is?"

"Goodness knows." Aisling suddenly remembered something and put her hand into her pocket. "I almost forgot—he gave me his card on the bus."

Seamus took it from her. "I won't ask what bus—I don't think I want to know. Hmm. Otis G. Weinberger. That doesn't tell us much."

"He was in John Smith's shop talking about

volcanoes and he spied on you in Dalkey and he was in Shetland and he followed me up here and knows all about you and S.K.U.N.K. And he's here now, just waiting for that boat to come in. He *must* be working for S.K.U.N.K."

Seamus looked thoughtful. "It'd do no harm to take a look in my rogues' gallery, I suppose." He rummaged through a pile of books and papers beside his bed until he found an old, dog-eared sketch pad. He opened it and leafed through it. "No sign of anyone resembling either of your descriptions. Look for yourself."

Aisling took the pad and searched through the sketches of various S.K.U.N.K. agents. She found Lerntowski and Shavitov, looking more like Laurel and Hardy than ever, but there was no trace of either Olga or Owl-face. "That doesn't prove anything," she said. "S.K.U.N.K. must be getting new people all the time. And you must admit it's fishy, them turning up here just when the boat's due to arrive."

"Ah yes. The boat. Have a look outside, child, and tell me what's happening."

Aisling opened the door and looked out. The *Fafnir* had dropped anchor in the bay and was bobbing gracefully on the sunlit water looking, with the sea and the Mountains of Mourne behind her, like something straight out of a film.

A dinghy was making for the shore. Three people were in it.

"It's too late," Aisling reported. "They've arrived. They'll be at the jetty in a minute."

"Go down and meet Thorwald and bring them up here."

"Please," Aisling muttered. She jumped out of the van and squeezed through the crowd to the quay, keeping well away from Chris, Olga and Owl-face. The smaller figure in the boat threw her a rope and she managed to tie it to a mooring-ring. Two men and a boy stepped ashore.

"Excuse me, are you Mr...Thorwaldson?" Aisling was relieved she'd managed to remember his name.

The taller of the two men, a huge grey-haired giant of a man with a bushy grey beard and ice-blue eyes, smiled down at her. "I am he."

"I'm Aisling, Seamus's goddaughter. He asked me to bring you to him immediately."

"Seamus is here? Good."

There was hardly room inside the removals van for the two men, the boy and herself, but Aisling was determined to squeeze in and hear what happened.

Seamus and Thorwald greeted each other in what she supposed was Norwegian, and then Thorwald introduced his two companions. "This is my first mate, Archie, and my son, Erik."

Archie was a stocky little man with flaming red hair and freckles, about the same age as her father, Aisling thought. And Erik was about her own age. He had very fair hair, which he wore short, and the same ice-blue eyes as his father. He was quite good-looking, she thought, in a sulky sort of a way.

"Well, my friend," Thorwald said. "I am here. What is this idea of yours?"

Seamus's eyes twinkled. "How do you fancy a trip to Iceland?"

"To Iceland? You are going crazy, old friend. I have come on a courtesy visit to Man with a small crew—to go on a major voyage, even in summer, we need more crew and more time. I have neither. One should not attempt to build a tent with only one reindeer hide."

"Norway has had earthquakes too. And volcanic activity in the Arctic Circle," Seamus pointed out.

"Yes. We have had earthquakes. Very bad ones."

"The bunch of megalomaniacs who are behind them are in Iceland now. We have to stop them. And for that, I need your ship."

"We, my friend? Let the governments stop them. One does not keep a team of dogs and pull the sleigh oneself."

"They are threatening to split the Atlantic Ocean right down the middle. And I fear they have the means to do it. Will you just stand aside and let them? They won't stop till the whole world is destroyed."

"Perhaps the world is destined to be destroyed?"

"Perhaps. But not yet. And not by a bunch of morons like S.K.U.N.K. Think of the effect it'll have, man. Not only on people, but on whole continents, on mountain ranges, on wild life. Every living thing in the sea for miles on either side of the fault will be killed for a start."

Thorwald was silent.

Seamus tried a different tack. "Do you remember that trouble up in Trondheim in 1964? Lerntowski was behind that—and he's behind this mess now."

"Lerntowski." Thorwald said the name quietly, but the menace in his voice made Aisling shiver.

"Exactly. I helped you there, Thorwald. I need your help now."

Thorwald puffed thoughtfully on his pipe for a long while. There was silence inside the van (apart from a crunching noise from near the driver's end, where Mulligan, having found a packet of biscuits, was having a snack to keep him going).

Then Thorwald turned to Archie. "Do you think we can make it?"

"Iceland? In yon wee boat? You must be mad!"

Thorwald looked back at Seamus with a smile. "There. You see."

"We'll make it. We have to make it. Yours is the only ship that will." A thought struck him. "What type of rivets did you use?"

"Rivets?"

"*Rivets*, man! For keeping your planks together!"

"Wooden ones. The *Fafnir* is modelled on an East Baltic merchant ship."

Seamus let out his breath in a long sigh. "That's what I hoped. Now, how many more men do you need?"

"You are coming yourself?"

Seamus looked at him levelly. "If you will take me. I'll need a bed and I'll be no help to you physically. But perhaps my mind may be of some use."

"If it is Lerntowski we are up against, it is your mind we will need. And yes, we can make room for you on the ship."

"Are you stark staring bonkers?" Archie burst out. "Taking a wee boat to Iceland wi' an auld cripple and a bed on it, and that wi' not even a proper cabin! It's no a luxury cruiser, ye ken, it's a primitive mode of transport we're talking aboot."

Thorwald ignored him. "We will rig an awning at the stern and lay your mattress under it. And we will hope for calm seas." He smiled. "Florence, and I hope Florence is with you, old friend, can sleep in the cabin I have built in the cargo hold. The Vikings themselves, as far as we know, slept on the open deck, but I am not so young as I was: a young sapling can withstand the storm, but an old fir tree survives better sheltered from the wind."

"Florence?" Archie sounded horrified. "You're no thinking of taking a wumman on board, are ye?"

"Florence is an unusual woman, my friend. It is prudent to refrain from judging the wine until you have tasted it."

"It's no' prudent to allow a wumman on board a ship," Archie stated firmly.

"Aisling. Will you please go and fetch

Christopher?" Seamus adroitly changed the subject. Aisling grinned and went out onto the quay.

She found Chris gazing at Olga like a pup waiting for a stick to be thrown. Owl-face was standing beside them, a quiet smile on his lips.

Chris turned to her, his eyes shining. "Hey, Ash! Isn't it fantastic! Olga and Otis are both great sailors! They're both dying to try sailing on a real Viking ship!"

I'll bet they are, thought Aisling grimly. "Seamus wants to see you," she said.

"Fine." He turned to the others. "Wait here. I won't be long. I'll see if I can wangle a passage for you both."

Aisling stayed outside the van this time, to make sure that neither Owl-face nor Olga tried to eavesdrop on the planning inside. She looked at them sourly: dying to sail in a Viking ship, her aunt Fanny! Seamus would soon put paid to that idea.

But when Chris came back his face was shining. "Great news! You're both coming with us!"

Aisling froze. "They're from S.K.U.N.K.!" she hissed.

Chris looked at her pityingly. "Seamus said you thought that. You're going paranoid, Aisling my love. Olga is on our side, fighting S.K.U.N.K. And she's a first-class experienced sailor. Otis knows how to sail too. As Thorwald needs more crew, it's worked out fantastically."

"You're an idiot," said Aisling angrily. "And I am not your love. Excuse me."

She stormed into the van. "They're spies! You know they are! We can't take them with us!"

"Who said anything about we?"

"Please, Seamus. I've come this far. And Mum's not expecting me home for at least a couple of weeks. And I won't get in the way. I've done some sailing too—I'll bet I'm as good as that Olga woman. I can't believe you really mean to take her."

Seamus smiled infuriatingly. "We need Christopher to help crew the boat. And he won't come without his latest girlfriend. So what can I do?"

"Rats. I don't believe you. You'd never let anything like that make a difference."

"Maybe not. But what else do you suggest? If she is a S.K.U.N.K. agent—and we've still no definite proof of it—she's seen the *Fafnir* and she'll have realized why I want it."

"Why do you want it? A destroyer is a million times bigger and stronger than the

Fafnir, and I've seen what happens to destroyers when they get near Iceland: they start coming to bits. How on earth can a museum piece like that do any better?"

"Because that museum piece, as you put it, is fixed together with wooden rivets."

Seamus looked at her smugly, waiting for her to ask what difference that made. She tried to find an answer so as to avoid giving him the satisfaction, but couldn't see any connection.

"*Wooden* rivets." Seamus stressed the word.

"So?"

"Seamus sighed. "What are rivets usually made of?"

"I don't know. Iron or steel, I suppose."

"Exactly."

"I still don't get it."

"The *Fafnir* has no iron or steel." Seamus spoke slowly and precisely, like someone doling out sweets to greedy children. "Or, if it has, they shouldn't be holding anything vital together. Are you getting warm?"

"The magnetic shield works like a magnet and magnets only affect iron! Of course!"

"Hmm. So they do teach you something in that school of yours."

"And you think Olga will have worked that

out as well?"

"Not everyone is as slow as yourself."

"Thanks," said Aisling. "But if she knows why you're using the boat, she'll tell S.K.U.N.K. and they'll be waiting for us."

"True. Can you think of a way of stopping her?"

We could murder her, Aisling thought. *Unidentified body of woman washed up on Irish coast...* Except that she couldn't see Seamus or Florence or Chris committing murder in cold blood. Thorwald maybe, she thought with a shudder. "Can't we hand her over to the police?" she asked.

"On what charge?"

"I don't know. I'm sure you could think of one."

"Not one that would stick. And she's a foreign national: there'd be a dreadful fuss. No, she's safe with us. That way, we can keep an eye on her."

"I suppose you're right." Aisling was still very doubtful. And then another thought struck her. "I suppose that goes for Owl-face too?"

"If you mean our friend Otis. Obviously."

"Rats and double rats," said Aisling. "This trip is going to be fun."

12
Olga

hey set sail in the early evening. There was just enough breeze to ruffle the water and fill the large woollen sail. Looking ahead, past the carved dragon on the prow, Aisling and Mulligan watched the coast of Northern Ireland pass slowly by, glowing in the long golden rays of the evening sun. Small white-washed houses clung to the shore; a car glinted as it sped along the coast road; cattle—small dark dots—grazed peacefully on patch-work pastures.

Later, Aisling went below to help Florence make supper. The cabin was just a rough wooden shelter over a hole in the deck, with room below for a tiny galley, complete with stove and table, and a few narrow bunks. The floor was so near the sea that it was like being pulled along underneath the waves in a thin wooden box.

They ate on deck. Aisling hadn't realized how hungry she was: even if she'd been served up cold porridge, she felt, she'd have gulped it down—and the meal Florence had come up with was, as usual, fantastic. She sometimes thought Florence would have managed to cook a *cordon-bleu* meal over a bundle of sticks in a cave, if she'd been born in the Stone Age.

The sun sank lower on the horizon and the sea became streaked with blood. As dusk fell, Archie brought out his mouth organ and started playing it softly. The seagulls were silent, the waves splashed against the side of the hull, the sail flapped gently in the wind. If Mulligan hadn't been jumping about all over the place trying to catch the moths attracted by the lantern Archie had hung from the cabin roof, it would have been idyllic.

Aisling looked back at the black shadow on their left, which was all that was left of Ireland. Port, she told herself. I must remember. Although she'd told Seamus she knew about boats, she'd only been on one once, as a passenger on the sailing boat belonging to her friend Louise's father: they'd crossed Dublin Bay from Dun Laoghaire to Howth and

back, and all she'd ever had to do was to duck
when she'd been told to, to avoid the boom. At
least the Viking sail didn't swing round and
hit you on the head all the time.

Florence stood up to clear away the plates.

"Yon was a grand meal," said Archie
appreciatively. "Tho' I canna' say I enjoy haein'
wumman on ma' boat," he glared at Olga,
curled up companionably beside Chris, "I'm
fair delighted we took you wi' us, Florence. I
hanna' eaten as good as this since I left
hame—and that wisna' yesterday."

Florence, to Aisling's surprise, blushed.

"A woman who can cook is worth twenty
creels of herring," Thorwald commented.

Owl-face (she'd have to get used to calling
him Otis, Aisling thought glumly) stood up
and took the tray from Florence. "Allow me,
ma'am." He looked round at the others. "I
suggest we introduce a non-sexist implement-
ation into the parameters of domestic activities.
It would be wrong, equality-wise, for the ladies
to do all the housework. I, for example, will do
the washing up tonight."

Erik, who was sitting near Aisling, still
eating the last piece of chicken (with his
fingers, she noticed), muttered something. It
sounded like "Women are a curse on a ship at

any time." She glared at him. He really was horrid.

He noticed her look, ran his greasy fingers through his hair and grinned at her. She turned away. She wished Mulligan would do the same, but he seemed to have taken a fancy to Erik and had sat by him all meal, looking longingly into his face and sitting up on his heavy hindquarters to beg whenever Erik looked as if he might throw him a crumb. When Aisling had tried to tempt him away with a piece of chicken skin, which was all she had left, he'd ignored her, preferring to wait for the odd piece which Erik had casually given him. She wished, almost, that she'd left him with Mrs Byrne in Dalkey.

Thorwald split the crew into two watches: himself, Chris and Olga in one; Archie, Otis, Erik and herself in the other. "For the moment at least," he said. "When I see how you all manage, we will rearrange the watches so that we shall all have more time off. It is better to observe first how well a man works before allowing him to guard your herd."

"Thorwald's crazy," she told Seamus when she brought him his evening mug of cocoa. She sat beside him under the tarpaulin which had been rigged over his mattress and looked forwards to where Olga and Chris were standing very close together in the moonlight. "They're going to be soppy all voyage. Why didn't he put me with Chris? I'm stuck with that ghastly boy, Erik."

"Poor you."

Aisling glared at him. "Thanks for the sympathy."

"What do you expect? Here, take this mug back. And move that orange monstrosity—this bed's not big enough for that lump of over-fed cat-flesh and myself."

Biting back a retort, Aisling picked up Mulligan and the mug and turned to go.

"You forgot to say 'Goodnight, godfather'," Seamus mocked.

"'Night," she muttered, without turning round. "And I hope you get eaten by mosquitoes," she added under her breath.

She passed Olga and Chris on the way back to the makeshift cabin. "I'll take your mugs." Purposely, she stepped between the two of them. Mulligan, on her shoulder, brushed against Olga's arm. The Russian drew back with a shudder.

Aisling suppressed a grin. "Oh, Olga—did you meet Florence's cat? He loves being tickled under the chin."

Olga backed against the side of the boat. "Take heem avay. Cats are no good. I hates zem."

"It's just because you're not used to them." Aisling moved Mulligan forwards in her arms and held him out to Olga. "Just pet him. He won't scratch."

Mulligan's legs were dangling in the air and Seamus's mug was digging into his ribs. On top of this, he was being thrust at a person who obviously didn't like him. He growled viciously and spat as he struggled to get down. Aisling, smiling sweetly, held him tight and pushed him even closer to Olga.

"Take heem avay!" she screeched.

"Honestly, Aisling." Chris put his arm protectively round Olga's shoulders. "You can see Olga doesn't want him. Stop being a nuisance and just get lost, will you."

"Sorry. I didn't realize she was so neurotic." Aisling hoisted Mulligan back over her shoulder and went triumphantly below. Chris could be as angry as he liked—nobody in their right minds would want to love someone who was scared of cats. She'd keep on showing Olga up until Chris saw some sense at last.

She settled Mulligan on her bunk and climbed under the blankets.

She was woken by Erik shaking her shoulder roughly. "Come. It is late."

She groaned and looked at her watch: one a.m.!

Archie and Otis were already on deck drinking mugs of coffee. Thorwald was still there too. "Seamus tells me you know how to sail, little one."

Aisling avoided his eye. She thought of trying to bluff, but realized immediately that it wouldn't work: anyone could tell in ten seconds that she knew nothing about boats. "Well...no. Not really," she admitted. "But I'm a quick learner. Just tell me what to do and I'll do it."

Archie snorted. "Ah'm expected to be a nursemaid noo, am I?"

Thorwald patted him on the shoulder. "The weather is calm—the *Fafnir* is easy to sail at present. And a willing learner is better than a stubborn mule. Erik will teach her what she needs to know."

Erik groaned audibly, and then quickly bent down to tickle Mulligan, who was rubbing around his ankles. But Aisling had heard him. It was bad enough having to admit she knew nothing; having to take orders from a ghastly boy who thought he knew it all made it a thousand times worse. The time, the lack of sleep, the cold and Mulligan's desertion did nothing to improve her spirits.

Thorwald's watch went below and Archie ordered Erik to show Otis and herself the ship while he took charge of the steering. Otis had obviously sailed before: he made sensible remarks, asked intelligent questions and soon gained Erik's respect. She, on the other hand, was made to feel more and more stupid. Erik was obviously enjoying showing her up.

Rats, she thought. He'll see. *Dublin schoolgirl saves replica Viking ship single-handed!* Just give her time.

Each watch lasted three hours: by the time it was their turn on deck again, the sun was burning through the morning mist and it was promising to be another brilliant day. Aisling spent most of the watch looking at the coastline passing by.

Sometimes forests cascaded down from the summit of hills like a black lava flow; in other places the hills were covered in fields or stretches of purple heather; occasionally trees crawled along the skyline like a chain of blind men leaning on each others' shoulders; roads sneaked across the side of the hill; a caravan park full of caravans and cars like rows of cardboard cartons appeared at the head of a bay; golden-yellow, dark-green, grey-yellow fields stretched up behind it; cars, like boxes on a conveyor belt, slid behind bushes, walls, fences with the sun glinting on silver, making white brighter, shimmering the red. The dragon prow of the Viking ship cut through the waves, throwing white spume back on either side.

Aisling Daly, Viking adventuress, leads her fleet of longships to raid an Irish monastery!

By afternoon, the novelty had worn off and she looked for something to do. She remembered a shelf of books in the cabin: she would go down and see if there was anything worth reading.

She was in bare feet and made no sound as she approached the steps leading down to the cabin. Everyone else was on deck, talking or sunbathing or finishing the afternoon tea which Florence had provided. (Otis's idea about job-sharing hadn't lasted long, she thought with a grin: his conscience seemed to trouble him as little as that of the other male members of the crew—or her own or Olga's either, for that matter—when Florence offered to do all the household chores.)

Something made her stop. She listened.

From below the wooden cover, she heard a faint tapping. Careful not to make a sound, she crouched down and peered into the gloomy interior.

At first she could see nothing after the bright sunlight outside, but there was definitely a tapping noise coming from one of the bunks in the far corner. Dot...dot...dash... It was morse! Someone was signalling!

She leapt down the steps and pulled the curtain back from the bunk. Olga's eyes blazed up at her. "You fool!" she hissed. She pushed Aisling back against the opposite bunk and, in one quick gesture, threw a blanket over something in the bed. But not before Aisling had seen what it was: a small black box with wires and dials. Olga had been using a radio transmitter!

"I knew it!"

Olga grabbed her by the arm. "You know nozink!" Her black eyes flashed and her long red nails dug into Aisling's skin.

Aisling pulled herself free and backed towards the steps. Olga followed her. One of Florence's kitchen knives was lying on the galley table. Both of them noticed it at the same time. Olga's hand went out.

There was an orange flash, a thump and

Mulligan stood on the table, his nose sticking into Olga's face, an expectant look in his big yellow eyes. He had followed Aisling down to the cabin in the hope of getting some more food, and now this strange woman was going to feed him instead. He was delighted.

Olga jumped back in disgust.

Aisling grabbed her chance and rushed up the steps. "Help! Thorwald! Chris! Help!"

Chris jumped up and ran towards her. "What's happened?"

Olga's after me with a knife! She wants to kill me!"

Chris let go of her abruptly. "Very funny. I am sick fed up of you being nasty to Olga. If you can't be polite, just leave her alone."

Aisling turned to Thorwald. "Olga's got a radio transmitter down there. She was sending a message to S.K.U.N.K. I heard her."

"So?" Thorwald looked grim. "Come."

Olga had replaced the knife and was at the tiny mirror, putting on lipstick. She smiled at Thorwald as he came down the steps. "Captain! How arrre you? Can I get you somezink?"

"You have a radio transmitter?"

"Radio transmitter? What for would I hav zat?" Olga looked a model of surprised innocence.

"It's in her bunk." Aisling pushed past them and pulled back the cover. There was nothing there.

Thorwald stroked his beard. "Shall we go back on deck?"

"But..."

Thorwald silenced here with a glance. He waited for her to go up the steps first. Seething, she went straight to Seamus.

"Hmm." Seamus scribbled on his pad. "Did her machine look like that?" Aisling nodded. "You were right, then. It is a radio transmitter. I wonder who she was trying to contact?"

"S.K.U.N.K., of course."

"Perhaps. Ah, Thorwald. Just the man I wanted to see. Aisling here's a bit bored. I suggest you put her to tidying out the cabin."

"But Florence did that al... " She realized what Seamus was getting at and stopped.

Thorwald smiled. "A good idea, my friend. Yes. There are more ways than one of skinning a rabbit."

"Keep Olga and Otis away, then."

Seamus smiled. "Ask our two foreign guests to join us, Thorwald. I feel like a game of cards." As Olga, dressed today in an emerald green sun top and exceedingly short shorts, came up on deck again, his eyes twinkled. "A bit of feminine company will do an old man good."

Aisling couldn't help grinning. "At your age! I'm ashamed of you."

Mulligan was still in the cabin when she returned. She gave him some food to keep him quiet and then started on a systematic search. It wasn't easy. The cabin was incredibly cramped and Florence's provisions were packed into every available space. She became more and more discouraged. Olga must have hidden the transmitter somewhere, but where? There was certainly no room in what she was wearing to hide anything larger than a grain of rice.

Footsteps approached the cabin, legs appeared and Archie came down the steps. His face went scarlet when he saw what Aisling was doing. "Why, you thieving wee rascal! What the hell are ye up to? That's ma locker!"

"Sorry." Aisling backed away hastily. She explained what she was doing. At first Archie didn't believe her but, when he heard that Thorwald himself had given her permission to search, he changed his mind. "I never did like yon painted hussy. It widna' surprise me if she was up to nae guid. Did you look behind the bulkhead?"

"The what?"

He pulled her out of the way, reached down behind one of the bunks and unscrewed a panel. "Aye. That's where she has it."

He withdrew the small metal box Aisling had glimpsed before. He examined it carefully. "Hmm. Albanian. That would figure. Come on, lass—we'd better show this to Thorwald."

The colour left Olga's face when she saw the transmitter in Archie's hand, but otherwise she didn't move a muscle. "Two spades," she said calmly.

Seamus sat up straighter in bed and grinned from ear to ear. He looked like Mulligan after a plateful of liver, Aisling thought. "Well? What have you to say now?" he asked Olga.

"I hav said eet. Two spades."

"Dinna haver, wommun. We've found your radio."

Olga put down her cards and looked at the machine in Archie's hands. "I do now know vat ees zees zing."

"You rotten liar!" Aisling burst out. "I saw you with it!"

Olga turned her black eyes innocently up to Thorwald. "I do not know vat zey arrre talking about."

"The locked stable door stops a second horse escaping." Thorwald took the transmitter from

Archie and handed it to Seamus. "Perhaps you should look after this, old friend."

Seamus pushed it down under the bedclothes to the foot of the bed where it formed a square bump beside the two smaller humps of his feet. "That should at least stop that damned orange feline from sitting on me." He grinned at Olga. "Two spades, you said?"

Olga stood up. "I hav feenished. Zees game ees borring." She walked over to the rail and put her arm round Chris.

"I told you," Aisling said smugly. "I knew she was a spy. And now they know we're coming and they're expecting us. What are we going to do?"

Seamus put the cards back in their box. "There's nothing we can do. So forget it, and enjoy the trip."

"But..." Aisling appealed to Thorwald. "Can't you lock her up or something?"

He smiled down at her. "Where, Aisling? We have no prison here. Remember, an enemy known is an enemy halved. Your godfather is right: fate will decide what is to happen. We can do no more."

13
Submarine Ahoy!

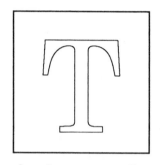 he fine summer weather continued and they sailed steadily northwards. As the days merged together, life on board the *Fafnir* settled into a routine. No-one mentioned the transmitter again, although the bump at the foot of Seamus's bed was a constant reminder, and the men in the crew continued to drool over Olga—to Aisling's disgust. What made matters worse was that, not only did the S.K.U.N.K. spy look like a film star and dress like a mannequin modelling "What to wear on a cruise this summer," but she was also a very good sailor.

It was highly unfair. Erik was the world's worst show-off and never failed to score off her, and Archie, Thorwald and Seamus all treated her like a kid. The only ones that tried to be

friendly to her were Olga and Otis—and that
was because they both belonged to S.K.U.N.K.
Even Mulligan spent more time with Erik
than he did with her. And then people blamed
her for being sulky. She sometimes wished
she'd never come.

On the sixth day out, the wind dropped
completely.

"Are we going to have to start rowing?"
Aisling asked Archie when the *Fafnir* hadn't
moved for at least an hour.

"Fit dae ye think this is, lassie? She's a
merchant ship, no' a warship. Did ye no notice
we hae oarholes only in the bow and the stern,
no a' the way along the sides? That's so's we
can manoeuvre if we hae to land in a dangerous
place. Otherwise, we jist sit patiently and wait
for the wind."

The wind was a long time in coming. As the
day wore on with the sun beating down on the
motionless ship, tempers began to fray.

Seamus became more and more crotchety.
He sat up in bed in his shirtsleeves, scratching
viciously with a piece of charcoal on his
sketchpad: drawings of boats, motors,
windmills, tornadoes, even sandstorms piled
up on the duvet around him, covering Mulligan
(who still found room for himself on the bed

despite the radio transmitter at the foot of it)
like leaves on a dead hedgehog. Mulligan
continued to snore gently.

Archie and Otis were fishing from the stern.
Every now and again their lines would tangle
and Archie would let out a stream of rich and,
to Aisling, quite unknown swearwords. Otis
just smiled his hesitant smile, untangled the
lines and cast his spinner out again. Erik was
fishing too, but had stationed himself well out
of their way and was lashing the water angrily
with a string of mackerel feathers. None of
them had caught anything, which didn't help.

Florence had brought her knitting up on
deck and was sitting contentedly chatting to
Thorwald as he puffed at his pipe. The only
other people on the ship who seemed unaffected
by the delay were Chris and Olga, and that
was because all Chris wanted to do, Aisling
thought nastily, was to stare adoringly into
Olga's eyes, and all Olga wanted to do was be
stared at. It was enough to make anyone sick.

She was also becoming bored with sunbathing. She went down to the galley to look
for some scraps for the gulls. For a moment she
watched them gliding behind the ship, like
snow-white chubby torpedoes with wings, until
the weight of their bodies dragged them

seawards; then, just as it looked as if they were going to crash into the water, they tilted their heads and, still without moving their wings, soared upwards again.

Then she threw a scrap of fat into the air. Immediately, half a dozen birds slipped suddenly sideways, swooped, pecked at it and soared up again, the losers kak-kak-kaking as they mobbed the one who had caught the fat. She threw some more, enjoying their airborne ballet. More gulls arrived to see what they could get. The raucous screeching rose to new levels.

Mulligan heard them. He raised his head, scattering paper all over the bed, narrowed his yellow eyes to baleful slits and glared at them.

Just to annoy him, Aisling came nearer to Seamus's bed. She threw some more scraps into the air. The seagulls screeched and screamed overhead and then swooped down alongside the bed, practically touching it with their outstretched wings. It was too much.

With a spring that made Seamus swear violently as his ribs bore the full brunt of Mulligan's powerful back legs, Mulligan threw himself at the nearest herring gull.

He had forgotten that he was so close to the edge of the boat. To Aisling's horror, he sailed straight over the side.

"Help!" she screamed.

Erik dropped his line and raced over. Below them, Mulligan's head appeared in the sun-dappled water. Erik kicked off his runners and dived into the sea. Aisling remembered the lifebelt Thorwald kept attached to the mast and she flung it after him. Erik grabbed Mulligan, who dug his claws into his neck, yowling pitifully (or more likely angrily, knowing Mulligan, Aisling couldn't help thinking). As soon as Erik had managed to grab the lifebelt with his free hand, Aisling pulled it in. By this time, everyone had crowded round the side of the boat. Someone dropped Erik a rope. Aisling watched in grudging admiration as he clambered back on board despite Mulligan hanging onto him like some monster from the deep, his claws drawing thin streaks of blood through Erik's shirt.

Erik crouched down on the deck and Aisling unhooked Mulligan as gently as possible. Looking like an oversized orange rat, with his fur plastered to his body and his tail, now thin as a rope, between his legs, Mulligan gave them all a filthy look, turned and dived into the cabin where a clatter of falling dishes announced his arrival.

Florence had the first-aid box ready. Aisling helped her to clean up the long ragged scratches on Erik's neck and shoulders. The antiseptic made him wince. He turned his head away so that she couldn't see the tears in his eyes. She felt awful. "I'm sorry." It seemed a terribly weak thing to say. "You were fantastic. You saved his life!"

Erik shrugged, and winced again. He forced a smile. "He would probably have saved himself anyway. Most cats can swim very well. And I'm sure, once he realized there was nothing to eat down there, he'd have managed to climb back up the side again, one way or another."

Aisling had to admit to herself that, when he smiled, Erik was actually quite good-looking. She smiled back. "Probably," she agreed. "But thanks anyway."

Erik went below to find dry clothes. To her surprise, when he came back on deck again he suggested she joined him fishing. She felt that, after what he'd done, she couldn't very well say no. Maybe it was because she actually could fish, having had plenty of practice with her father on holidays in the west, but Erik didn't seem quite so horribly superior now and she found herself enjoying his company. The only annoying thing was that Thorwald and

Florence were watching them with smug I-told-you-so faces. Rats, she thought.

Everyone was glad when the wind returned and the *Fafnir* started to move again. Soon they had left Scotland behind and were heading directly for Iceland. Cloud patterns and sea patterns took the place of hills and coastlines.

The seagulls now began to fall away. Gannets—huge brilliantly white birds with black-tipped wings—became more numerous, hurtling like thunderbolts down into the sea to catch fish with their vicious bills. Seals continued to appear, their black buoy-like heads bobbing out of the water to stare at the *Fafnir* with opaque glassy eyes. And now dolphins sometimes cavorted around the ship and once even a whale appeared.

Fishing boats, too, crossed their path, their crews staring in amazement at the Viking ship heading north in full sail. Some came in close for a better look and shouted ribald comments which Archie was well able to answer.

Aisling enjoyed these encounters as it meant a break from ship-board routine, but she gradually became aware that both Olga and Otis showed more interest in them than anyone else. She mentioned this to Seamus but was told to stop being paranoid. She kept a close watch all the same, to see if any of the fishing boats were exchanging signals with either of the spies: as far as she could see, none of them did.

And then, one night when she was on duty, a strange shape appeared in the sea. She pointed it out to Archie.

"That's a whale, lass. Have you no seen ane o' them before?"

"It's different," Aisling insisted. "It's too big." She appealed to Erik.

"Wait a minute. I'll get the binoculars."

He focussed them on the object, a black shape barely visible in the distance against the dark sea and the pale midnight sky. "Aisling's right!" His voice rose in excitement. "It's a submarine!"

"Here, gie me yon." Archie took the binoculars and studied the distant object. "Aye, so it is. But that's naething to get excited aboot. It'll be ane o' thae NATO subs—or maybe a Russkie. It's no uncommon to see submarines up here, ye ken."

"Say, guys. Mind if I have a look, momentarily-wise?" Nobody had heard Otis come up.

Aisling grabbed the glasses from Archie before Otis could get them. "I haven't had a turn." She had no intention of letting Otis have them back as long as the submarine was there.

But she was outwitted. A light shone out suddenly from the submarine. It flashed again. Then the sub sank slowly under the sea.

"That was a signal!"

"Aye. Mebbe."

"It was! S.K.U.N.K. was signalling to Otis here. Please, Archie, can't we lock him up somewhere before he gets a chance to signal back?"

Archie looked embarrassed. He smiled apologetically at Otis. "She's just got ower much imagination. Dinna mind her."

Otis didn't seem bothered. "As Thorwald might say, it's wise to engage in alert mental thinking in the present dangerous-situation situation. I'm glad she's on the ball."

"Weel, it's guid o' ye to tak it like that." Archie gave Aisling a disapproving look and stumped off.

She leant against the dragon head and stared out to sea. It was maddening that no one would believe her.

Erik came and stood beside her. "I think you are right. That submarine was signalling. What will we do?"

"I wish I knew what it meant. Two flashes.

That could mean anything. Otis didn't signal back, did he?"

"No. Unless...unless it was a prearranged message: I'll be back at two o'clock or something?"

"That's it! But we'll be off duty then."

"So will Otis. We'll just have to watch. If he goes up on deck, we'll follow him and see what happens."

Normally, Aisling fell asleep immediately, especially if she'd been on the first night-watch. Now, even with her hairbrush and a runner stuffed underneath her pillow to make it as uncomfortable as possible, it was difficult to keep her eyes open...

It seemed like only minutes later that Erik shook her awake. "Otis has gone," he whispered. "Come on!"

They tiptoed out on deck. It was a bright moonlit night and Aisling felt very visible as she left the shelter of the cabin, but Thorwald's watch were all drinking coffee beside Seamus's bed and fortunately no one looked their way. Otis was at the prow alone, staring out to sea.

Suddenly light flashed from a powerful torch in his hand: long, long, long; short, long, long; a pause; long; long, long, long; another pause; short, long, long, short; long, long,

long...

"Come on!" hissed Aisling. "We've got to stop him!" She raced along the deck and flung herself at Otis, knocking his torch into the sea.

"Why, you little..." The shy, half-humourous look had disappeared from Otis's face. For the first time, Aisling saw him look really angry. He grabbed her shoulders and shook her.

"What the hell do you think you're doing? That submarine is here on a matter of maximum importance, national-security-wise."

Aisling pulled free. "You're a spy! You were trying to warn S.K.U.N.K. that we're coming. At least Thorwald and Seamus will believe me now and lock you up or something."

Otis took a deep breath and smiled a rather grim smile. "I keep trying to communicate to you, Aisling, I am not working for S.K.U.N.K. If you really want to know who I am, loyalty-wise, I'm working for the CIA. If your godfather didn't have such a problem with conceptualizing an on-going interaction situation inter-nationally-wise, if he worked with us instead of maximising his individualistic parameters, like some geriatric superman, it wouldn't have been necessary to send a submarine to discover what he was up to, anti-S.K.U.N.K.-wise."

Thorwald strode over to find out what was

going on. He frowned at Aisling and Erik. "What are you two doing here? You should be in bed. You know the old saying: sleep while you can to gain strength for when you can not. Off with you."

"Otis is a spy! He was signalling to a submarine. We..."

"Did you hear what I said?" Thorwald's eyes flashed dangerously. "Bed!"

"Come on, Aisling." Erik pulled her away. "There's no point in arguing with father when he's angry," he advised her when they were out of earshot. "It's never any use."

"What are we going to do, though? We have to tell them what Otis was up to. Or did you believe all that stuff about the CIA?"

"That's the Central Intelligence Agency, isn't it—the American secret service? I suppose it's possible. He is American, after all."

Aisling groaned. "That's where S.K.U.N.K.'s so clever. They have agents in every country. Why does no one believe me he's a spy?"

Erik grinned. "I believe you, if that makes you happy. Or at least, I'll keep an open mind. I agree that we have to keep an eye on him."

A roar from Thorwald silenced them. "*Bed!*"

"Come on. We can't do anything more tonight, anyway."

"Nor can Otis," said Aisling sleepily. "At least, I hope not."

All the same, she was determined to stay awake, just in case the submarine came back and Otis tried to signal again.

But as soon as her head hit the pillow she was fast asleep, despite the hard lumps underneath it.

The next morning, Aisling told first Thorwald, then Seamus, Archie and Chris about Otis and the submarine, but none of them seemed to take it seriously. Otis himself behaved as if nothing had happened. She ate her breakfast in silence. *Irish schoolgirl knew two foreign agents were spies but nobody would believe her...* It was infuriating being the only one with any sense and having everyone treat you like a stupid child with too much imagination.

"What on earth are you sitting there like a broody hen on a batch of rotten eggs for, child?" Florence asked her. "Can't you at least be civil? It's a lovely morning."

Chris winked at Florence. "She's just tired, Flo. She was up all night chasing imaginary spies instead of getting her beauty sleep."

Aisling pushed her bowl away and stood up abruptly. "Just because you think the sun rises and sets on your Olga there, doesn't mean the rest of us have to be blind as well. Doesn't it worry you that they're trying to get through to S.K.U.N.K. to tell them we're coming? I'm fed up with the lot of you. Come on, Mulligan—let's go and do some work."

"Well!" Florence looked inquiringly at the others. "What was all that about?"

"Nothing, ma'am," said Otis smoothly. "She's just living through an on-going emotional-period-situation at this moment in time. She'll grow out of it."

Erik finished his breakfast and went to join Aisling at the far side of the cabin.

"A fat lot of good you were," she accused him. "You might at least have backed me up."

Erik looked serious. "I'm sorry. But, you know, you could be wrong. And we are all stuck on the ship until we reach Iceland so there's no point in starting a fight. We might as well just play along with them. For the time being, anyway."

Aisling, who had been clutching Mulligan tightly for comfort, let him go. He shook himself and slumped down on the deck between them.

"I wish you had waited before you did your rugby tackle last night," Erik said.

"But we had to stop him signalling."

"I know. It's just... It would have been nice to find out exactly what he was going to say."

"What d'you mean?"

"Well, he'd only got as far as OW to PO before you attacked. OW must be Otis Weinberger, and we don't even know who PO is."

"You could read the signal?"

"It was morse. It's quite simple really. And you have to know it to be a sailor."

Aisling thought for a moment the old superior Erik had come back. She hoped not. "Let's go and ask Seamus what he thinks," she suggested. "He might have an idea."

Mulligan followed them to the stern where Seamus was sitting up in bed finishing his second bowl of porridge. He leapt onto the duvet and positioned himself expectantly by Seamus's elbow, following every movement of the spoon with his eyes opened to huge black orbs and his tongue flicking in and out to lick the saliva from round his mouth.

"Get that vulture away from me! How can a man enjoy his breakfast with a rapacious monster like that drooling over every mouthful?"

Aisling ignored him. "What does PO mean?"

she asked.

He looked at her with one bushy eyebrow raised. "Usually post office. Sometimes I wonder if you're pulling my leg: no one can be that ignorant."

"I don't mean post office. What else does it mean?"

"Post-operative. Pretty objectionable. Pilot officer. Why do you ask?"

"That sub Otis was signalling to last night. He signalled OW to PO."

"He did?" Seamus pushed the tray down off his knees and sat up straighter in the bed. Mulligan immediately put both front paws on the tray to hold it steady and rasped his tongue round the porridge which was left, until the bowl looked as clean as if Florence had washed it. Seamus pretended not to notice.

"PO," he said thoughtfully. "Pass me my rogues' gallery. It's in that bag, there."

Aisling handed him the sketch-pad in which he kept his drawings of S.K.U.N.K. agents. He flicked through it. "No. Nothing there."

"It could have been the first two letters of the submarine's name," Erik suggested.

"True," Seamus answered. "But I doubt if that helps us much. *Polar Icecap*? *Poltergeist*? *Potemkin*? *Potomac*? *Potato*? The possibilities are endless." He scratched his head with a stick of purple pastel colour, leaving a punkish-looking streak in his hair. "No. Unless Otis himself volunteers to tell us, I think this message of yours will remain one of life's great unsolved mysteries."

"We don't think he managed to tell them anything," Aisling said, trying to get Seamus to be serious. "But he might try again."

"True." Seamus looked at her shrewdly. "What if he *is* working for the CIA? Have you thought of that?"

"He isn't. He's with S.K.U.N.K."

"How nice to be so young and so sure of yourself."

Aisling ignored the sarcasm. "Alright. Let's suppose he is working for the CIA, what would he be signalling a submarine for?"

"To ask for a supply of hamburgers and coke? He could be pining for a MacDonald's takeaway."

Not for the first time, Aisling felt like strangling her godfather. She remembered a favourite phrase of her personal development teacher. "You're just being intentionally obstructive."

"Your vocabulary is improving. As for the Americans, you told me yourself they want to drop a nuclear bomb on Iceland. But at the moment, they can't get near. They're just like spoilt children unable to play with their favourite toy."

"That still doesn't explain why a submarine should be following us and why Otis wanted to signal to it."

Seamus sighed. "If Otis is working for the CIA, he no doubt hopes we'll help him to find a way through the magnetic barrier for the American bomber planes. They would need to keep in touch with him to find out if he's managed it yet."

"And you think that's more likely than that he was trying to get a message through to S.K.U.N.K. so that they can stop us coming? I'm the one who's supposed to have the imagination around here." Aisling was disgusted. "I take it, then, you're going to do nothing about Otis. Just let him wander round the ship like Olga, signalling to whoever he pleases. Well, I'm glad it keeps you happy. I only hope you're as amused when S.K.U.N.K. captures us all in Iceland."

She picked up Mulligan and stamped off.

14
Arachne Spins a Web

he next night there was
a brilliant sunset. As the
sun drowned like a bright
red disk in the sea behind the northern horizon,
the clouds rolled and changed shape in all
shades of pink and purple and black. The
scarlet-painted waves heaved and fell as if
some immense monster was shaking itself on
the ocean floor. Gradually the colours faded
and darkness smothered the ship in a black,
starless, moonless shroud.

The storm which followed was terrifying,
even below deck where Aisling had been told
to remain. The ship rolled and pitched so badly
that she felt like a marble in a matchbox—only
marbles stay dry. The waves must have been
washing over the *Fafnir*'s deck: with each roll,
a cascade of foaming cold water crashed into

the cabin, soaking everything. At first, she took her turn in manning the hand pump or baling with a bucket, but very soon she felt so sick that all she could do was to climb into one of the top bunks with Mulligan and hope to die.

It was even worse there. The creaking and groaning of the planks behind her sounded as if the *Fafnir* was being torn apart. No matter how hard everyone worked, the water kept coming in. She wondered how long it could last. Florence's assurance that, as Viking ships had sailed to Greenland and even Canada in weather worse than this as long ago as the tenth century, *Fafnir* would manage fine, didn't convince her. *Replica Viking ship lost at sea. Irish schoolgirl hockey loses one of its most promising players...*

The storm lasted three days.

"She is a good ship. And I have a good crew," said Thorwald on the fourth day, when the sea had calmed and the sun, finally, appeared again. "As the saying goes: with good men and a stout vessel, what can prevail?"

"Not just good men." Chris put his arm round Olga. "Good women too."

Aisling felt sick again.

Seamus had been listening to the radio.

"That was no ordinary storm. They have measured movement along the Atlantic ridge of nearly nine on the Richter scale. S.K.U.N.K. is beginning to turn the screws."

"Do you think the world governments will give in before we get there?" Aisling asked.

Seamus shrugged. "Maybe. Maybe not. I propose we press on, anyway."

"We have lost much time, old friend," said Thorwald. And we have been blown to the west, so it will take longer to get there. But, if you think it worth continuing, the ship will make it."

"It is better to travel hopefully than to arrive," said Aisling, quoting her maths teacher.

Thorwald gave her a look. Aisling wondered if he realized she was being cheeky. She hoped not.

During the next few days, a stiff breeze filled the *Fafnir*'s large square sail and blew them ever further northwards. Aisling imagined the ship as it would look on a map— or as someone would see it from a satellite above the earth: a tiny black speck crawling northwards to...to what? Could radio waves pierce the magnetic barrier? Had either Olga's or Otis's message got through to S.K.U.N.K.? If so, S.K.U.N.K. must know they were coming.

She hoped Shavitov and Lerntowski were safely locked up in Shetland: they *must* have been caught at the airport that time. Or must they? You could never be certain with S.K.U.N.K. Maybe they weren't just a tiny black speck in the middle of a vast ocean after all: maybe they were more like a fly on the water, a fly heading straight into the jaws of a monstrous, ravenous spider.

One evening, when the crew were relaxing on deck, Aisling noticed a sudden flash in the sky to the east. She turned to Erik. "Did you see that? Somebody's letting off fireworks!"

Erik watched the bright red light arc into the sky, burn for a minute like a brilliant new star and then fall back into the sea. "Someone's fired a distress flare! South-south-east!" he shouted.

Seamus felt under his duvet and brought out Olga's radio. He turned the tuning knob. Crackles of static, some faint music, snatches of voices in foreign languages passing too quickly for Aisling to recognize any of them, and then he found what he was looking for.

"Mayday! Mayday!" crackled the radio.

Seamus turned the knob to *transmit*. *"Fafnir* calling! We are receiving you. What is your position? Identify yourself."

Thorwald had picked up one of Seamus's sketch pads and a charcoal pencil and, as the map references came over the radio, he noted them down. "Fine, *Arachne*. Message received and understood. We are coming as fast as we can to your assistance. Over and out."

Seamus put down the set and looked at Thorwald. "They say they are sinking fast. Can we get there?"

"Not easily. We shall have to turn about and tack across the wind. But, when men's lives are at stake, one does not think of ease or hardship. Call all hands on deck!"

It took them over an hour to beat their way across the darkening sea. Seamus tried to make contact with the distressed ship again, but couldn't raise it on the radio.

"Maybe she's sunk already," Aisling said.

"Maybe. And maybe not. Are you suggesting we forget about them?"

"No. I was just thinking…"

"Don't," Seamus advised, "if that's the best you can do."

As Aisling tried to come up with a suitably cutting reply, another flare curved into the sky and hung overhead. This time it was so close that the whole sea, *Fafnir*'s dragon head, her huge red and white sail, all were bathed in crimson. And ahead of them, a black squat shape on the water, lay the *Arachne*, the ship in distress.

It was a large motor cruiser—the sort of boat Aisling had seen now and again in Dun Laoghaire harbour or on family holidays down the west. She wondered what it was doing this far north. Maybe the crew hadn't heard about the troubles in Iceland and had been heading there for a holiday.

She remembered how Chris's aircraft had reacted when they got near the magnetic barrier: maybe they were near it now and that was why the *Arachne* had broken down. If so, they were lucky that the only boat which could still function properly with no metal parts just happened to be near enough to rescue them.

She wondered what the *Arachne*'s crew were thinking as the tiny Viking ship with its huge sail and threatening dragon prow bore down on it.

The *Arachne*, however, appeared to be deserted. Its engine was silent and it was drifting helplessly on the choppy sea. Aisling remembered the story of the *Marie Celeste*, the sailing ship which had been found long ago, deserted, in the strange area of sea off the coast of Florida called the Bermuda Triangle.

Nobody had ever discovered what had happened to the crew: the rescuers had found the table laid for a meal and the food still on the table, just waiting to be eaten, she remembered.

Archie threw a rope over the *Arachne*'s rail and pulled the *Fafnir* alongside. He climbed the ladder hanging down from the motor-boat and disappeared.

A couple of minutes later his head popped up above them again. "It's afa' strange. There's naebody here, but there's a gey funny box in the cabin. I think you should mebbe come up and hae a look."

Thorwald climbed up the ladder. Erik and Aisling followed close on his heels.

It *was* like the *Marie Celeste*. There were even mugs half-full of lukewarm coffee on the table in the cabin and, in an ashtray, a slim black cigar sent up a spiral of smoke.

"What's happened?" Aisling asked excitedly.

"I dinna like it," Archie said. "There's something afa' funny going on."

"You are vise not to like eet, my friend. Put your hands up, yes?"

Aisling recognised the voice and spun round in horror. Shavitov's vast bulk filled the doorway. And he was pointing a machine gun straight at them!

"Man, oh, man," Archie groaned. "We were daft nae to guess that something was up."

"It is the uncommon person who is never wise after the event," Thorwald said calmly. "When men are in distress, you do not think of treachery. Although," his blue eyes glared icily at Shavitov, "where S.K.U.N.K. is concerned, one should expect no better."

"You vill shut up, old man." Shavitov stood aside and motioned them out of the cabin. "Come."

Aisling looked at Thorwald, Archie and Erik: which one of them would try to grab the machine gun? Probably Archie, she thought. He was nearest.

Thorwald put a hand on her shoulder. "Even the Arctic wolf knows when to watch and wait, Aisling," he said quietly. "Have patience. He who bends today may stand upright again tomorrow."

"You vill stop zees muttering, yes?" Shavitov ordered. "Come. Or I vill feel you full of holes."

Archie, his hands on his head, went up on deck. Aisling followed him and Thorwald and Erik came after her. She looked down at the *Fafnir*, hoping that Seamus would have realized they'd been tricked and would have thought of some way of turning the tables on. S.K.U.N.K.

To her dismay, Florence, Otis and Chris were all standing behind Seamus's bed. They, too, had their hands on their heads. In front of them, holding another machine-gun in a very businesslike fashion, was Olga. At least Chris must finally realize who's side she's on, Aisling thought with a certain satisfaction.

She looked for Lerntowski. If Shavitov had escaped from Shetland, he must have done so too. She was right. He was leaning against *Arachne*'s rail, looking up to the northern horizon where the invisible sun now tinged the sky a bloody red.

"Ve shoot them now, no?" Shavitov asked eagerly.

Lerntowski turned slowly and looked at him out of cold pale eyes. "No. No bloodshed. You know I do not like the sight of blood."

Shavitov's face fell. Then he brightened up again. "Ve shall throw zem overboard, no?" He sounded like Mulligan begging for scraps, Aisling thought with a shudder. Mulligan! That gave her an idea. Where was he? Shavitov was highly allergic to cats. If Mulligan could be made to rub up against him and start him sneezing, he might drop the gun and someone might have a chance to rush him. She looked round the *Fafnir*'s deck. Why was it that when he was needed, he was never anywhere about?

"No. Put them all on the Viking ship." Lerntowski's glance travelled over them slowly, one at a time: Aisling, Archie, Thorwald, Otis, Erik, Florence and, last of all, Seamus sitting up in bed with a tartan rug over his shoulders and a knitted Norwegian cap on his head. "We shall give them a Viking funeral," he said in his high squeaking voice.

Shavitov shepherded them down the ladder onto the *Fafnir*'s deck. Olga, after a command in some foreign language from Lerntowski, disappeared below and came back with the rope Florence had hung from the mast to the rail on fine days to dry her washing. Cutting it into lengths, she tied them hand and foot, one after the other. Aisling waited for her turn to come. Why didn't someone *do* something? There were only three S.K.U.N.K. agents—no, four: someone had started the *Arachne*'s engine! But there were seven of them, including Seamus. Why were they all standing like hypnotised rabbits, just waiting to be trussed up and... She didn't know what Lerntowski was planning to do with them, but she was sure it was something terrible. He'd said he'd give them a Viking funeral, but what did that mean? She wished she'd paid more attention in National School when Miss O'Neill had done the Vikings.

Shavitov's attention had been distracted by Olga whispering in Chris's ear as she tied him up. Chris was nodding his head understandingly. The smile he gave her was as besotted as ever, Aisling thought. How could he be so wet?

But it might give her a chance... Shavitov couldn't look at all of them at once...

"I suggest you stay where you are, little girl." Lerntowski's squeaky voice stopped her before she had started to move. And he, too, had a machine-gun in his hands. As had the swarthy-looking seaman standing beside him.

Rats, Aisling thought as Olga came up behind her and roped her hands together so roughly that she winced in pain. Olga gave the rope another twist. "You arre a stupid leettle girl," she hissed as she swept Aisling's feet from under her to make her fall onto the deck. "You zought you were clevairrer than Olga. You zought you could spy on her. Now ve vill see who is the most clevairr."

Aisling was tempted to tell her to go jump in the Liffey but, catching Seamus's eye, she thought she'd better not. She stared at the *Fafnir*'s deck, concentrating on the knot holes, the grain of the wood, *anything* rather than what was happening to them.

Seamus's testy voice made her look up. "You won't win," he said grumpily. "You may have stopped us now, but you will never win."

Lerntowski looked down at him with a twisted smile. "You would like to think so, grandaddy. But you are wrong. Already, the governments of the world are ready to give in to our demands. In a few more days, we will have what we want. It is a pity you will not be around to see it, but life, as you English say, is like that."

"God help the world," Seamus grunted, "if a moron like you is going to run it. England stops at the borders of Wales and Scotland. I wouldn't expect your fat lapdog there to know a basic geographical fact like that, but I expected better of you."

Lerntowski's smile vanished. He snapped out a command to Olga, who climbed on board the *Arachne*. Shavitov, at another command from Lerntowski, lumbered down into the cabin. They heard various things being thrown about. And then the sound of sneezing! Mulligan flew up onto the deck as if shot from the mouth of a cannon, and tried to dive under Seamus's bed. He stuck his head under the edge of the mattress. His back legs scrabbled loudly on the deck as he attempted to push the rest of his large body into a non-existent space. Aisling couldn't help grinning as she watched his orange rump gyrate and his tail lash with the effort. Giving up, he withdrew his head, sprang in two huge jumps to the mast and raced up it until he reached the top where he clung, terrified, a swaying orange blob high above them.

Shavitov emerged more slowly from the cabin. He had an axe in his hand. His eyes were red and streaming and he was sneezing incessantly. In between sneezes, he hacked viciously at the mast: Sneeze—crash!—sneeze—crash! Aisling watched, horrified, as the metal bit deep into the wood. It was only going to take him minutes to chop it through. They'd be killed if it fell on them, and there was no way, tied hand and foot as they were, that they'd be able to avoid it.

Finally, with a tearing, groaning sound, the mast gave. After a long minute's indecision, when it didn't seem to be able to make up its mind which way to fall, it crashed away from them, wrenching the *Fafnir* with it so that

Aisling rolled helplessly into Seamus's bed. Chris and Archie rolled on top of her, crushing her beneath them.

"Get off, all of you!" she heard Seamus shouting. "What do you think this is? A rugby scrum?"

She felt the others rolling off her and struggled to sit up. There was a huge gap in *Fafnir*'s side, with the mast lying drunkenly across it. Had anyone fallen through it into the sea? She looked round worriedly. No, they were all there, though Erik had rolled further from them and was lying separately from the rest of them, near the cabin.

Then she remembered Mulligan. He had been on the mast. Where was he now? It was impossible to see over the side of the ship but, even if he'd managed to hold on when it was falling, the top end would be under water by now. Her heart sank as she realized he had probably been drowned. Poor Mulligan. After all he'd been through. And all because of that horrid bully, Shavitov.

Shavitov came up from the cabin again. He had a green jerrycan in his hand. He poured its contents liberally over the cabin roof, soaking the rigging and the sail tangled over the top of it. He was still sneezing, Aisling noted with satisfaction. He leered at them as they lay huddled round Seamus's bed. "Ve vill do zees slow, no? A leetle flame, valking *slowly* over ze deck. Zat vill give you time to zeenk how you should not have laffed at Shavitov, yes?"

He sprinkled a thin trail from the cabin to the far edge of the deck. "Soon ze Viking sheep will burn, no? Eet vill be like Lerntowski say— a Viking funeral. I vish you a good journey to Valhalla, my friends."

The strange sound he was making was an attempt to laugh through his sneezing, Aisling realized. He struck a match and lit the end of the trail. Then he jumped, with surprising agility for one so fat, onto *Arachne*'s ladder and climbed on deck. The motor boat's engine roared into life.

As the flame trickled across the deck to the cabin, the *Arachne* sped off towards the northern horizon.

Aisling looked at Seamus urgently. "What are we going to do? Think of something!"

"Who do you suppose I am? Houdini?" Seamus snorted. "Can any of you move?"

Aisling struggled with the ropes around her wrists. Olga seemed to have tied her especially tightly. The rope bit into her flesh and the more she struggled, the more it hurt. Her fingers and toes were beginning to feel numb. She wondered how long it would be before they fell off from lack of blood, as her mother always warned her would happen if she tied a bandage too tight. Come back, Mum: all is forgiven, she thought wryly. On the other hand, they wouldn't be around for long enough to find out—once the petrol trail reached the cabin, the whole ship would go up in flames. Being made all of wood had its disadvantages.

A movement near the cabin caught her eye. Erik was humping himself across the deck like an ungainly seal. She watched, fascinated, as he bumped nearer and nearer to the petrol trail. The flame was trickling towards him. Would he reach it before it reached the cabin? And, even if he did, how could he put it out with his hands and legs tied? Wouldn't he just catch fire himself? She shuddered. Part of her wanted to shut her eyes tight and not see; another part forced her to watch.

She saw Erik reach the flame just as it got to the cabin. With a last convulsive effort, he rolled on top of it. The cabin erupted in a bluish flame which, as Aisling watched in horror, spread over Erik's body. She turned away and buried her face in Seamus's duvet.

Poor Erik. At least he'd tried. And now they had to lie here, waiting to be burnt to death as well—or roll over to the gap in the *Fafnir*'s side and fall into the sea. She wondered which would be worse: to be burnt alive or be drowned, tied hand and foot like a dog in a sack.

And then she heard Seamus laugh.

Thorwald joined in.

"I kent there was something funny aboot yon flame!" Archie said disgustedly. "It was the way the wind was blowing, I couldna' smell it. Yon's nae petrol—yon's brandy! Whit a waste of guid liquor!"

"Trust that moron Shavitov not to know the difference between Courvoisier and diesel oil," said Seamus. "I've often wondered how S.K.U.N.K. got as far as it has, with him on their side."

"It's Mulligan you should be thanking," Florence informed him tartly. "If that fat lout had been able to smell, instead of having a sneezing fit, he'd have realized he'd taken my cooking brandy by mistake. We owe that cat a lot."

"Hmph," said Seamus.

"Cooking brandy!" Archie sounded horrified. "You dinna cook with guid brandy dae ye, wumman? And keep it in a jerrycan like yon?

That's sacrilege, that's what it is."

Aisling opened her eyes. Blue flames were still dancing across the top of the cabin like... Of course! Like brandy flames over the Christmas pudding! And the Christmas pudding never got burnt, did it? They were saved!

"Do not rejoice before your reindeer are all safely in your paddock," Thorwald said quietly. "These flames still burn. However, I have almost frayed the rope around my wrists...." He winced. "There! Now. Seamus, your knife please."

He searched deftly through Seamus's box of paints for the old Swiss army knife Seamus used for sharpening pencils and cut his feet free. He then grabbed the duvet off Seamus's bed and, almost in the same motion, wrapped it round Erik, smothering the flames. Then he quickly cut the rope round Florence's hands, gave her the knife and turned back to Erik.

As soon as Florence was free, she hobbled painfully through the licking blue flames down into the cabin and came back with the medicine chest.

"What about us?" Aisling asked Seamus. "Aren't they going to cut us free too?"

"Quiet child. Old cripples and young girls

are bottom of the list. It's time you realized that. And Erik may be burnt."

"Oh." Aisling hadn't realized. She wished she'd kept her mouth shut and waited patiently with Archie, Otis and Chris until Thorwald came to free them.

"Is Erik all right?"

"He's fine," Florence said. "He just has a small blister on his hand." She pushed a wisp of curly white hair back from her face. "What we all need is a nice cup of tea. I'll go and put the kettle on while you try to clear up the deck here. We'll all feel better when there's a bit more order around."

Chris came over and helped Aisling to her feet. "Are you okay?" he asked.

She rubbed her wrists. "Y...es. I think so." She looked at him. Poor old Chris, she thought. He must feel awful now Olga's proved herself a S.K.U.N.K. agent in front of us all. "I'm sorry about Olga...." she started.

"It doesn't mean anything," Chris said at exactly the same time.

"What doesn't mean anything?"

"Olga's only pretending to be on their side."

"Pretending?" Aisling asked incredulously.

"'Will you stop repeating everything I say like a ruddy parrot!"

"Sorry. But you can't really believe that. You must know by now she works for S.K.U.N.K. You can't be that gone on her."

"I am not gone on her. It's just the rest of you that are so prejudiced. Just because she's beautiful and charming and intelligent, you think she must be evil as well. I'm disappointed in you, Aisling."

"Oh I give up." Aisling turned away in disgust. "I'm going to help Florence make the tea."

15
Cavalry to the Rescue

lorence had been right: tea did make them all feel better. But it was difficult to feel optimistic sitting in the wreck of the *Fafnir* in the middle of an empty ocean, miles from the nearest land. Aisling found it hard not to cry.

She sniffed and put her hand out for her mug of tea. It hit something soft and furry.

She jumped. "Mulligan!" she yelled. "Mulligan's alive!"

"Have you just noticed?" Seamus asked sourly. "He's already scoffed the whole plateful of anchovy sandwiches Florence left on my bed. Being thrown overboard doesn't seem to have made the slightest difference to that fur-covered food-processor's appetite."

Aisling picked Mulligan up and hugged

him. He let her for a moment, poking his cold orange nose into her face and purring like a dentist's drill; and then he pulled himself away and went to sit on his hind legs in front of Otis who was eating the last of his sandwiches. There was a flash of orange paw, the last portion of sandwich leapt from Otis's fingers and Mulligan was chasing it across the deck to swallow it in one gulp. He jumped angrily aside as Otis swiped at him.

Erik rubbed the top of his head with a bandaged hand. "Thank goodness you're all right, Mulligan," he said fondly.

"Hmph," said Seamus and Otis together.

Mulligan looked at them all in turn, realized there was nothing more to eat, stalked with dignity over to Seamus's bed and sprawled across the foot of it. He closed his yellow eyes and went instantly to sleep.

"It's a great life for some," Seamus growled. But Aisling noticed he allowed Mulligan to stay there. "A pity we humans can't take life as easily. How soon do you think we can get under way again, Thorwald?"

Thorwald had been examining the broken mast. He looked grave. "I do not know, my friend. We have no spare mast. We can row, of course, but this is a merchant ship and not designed for rowing—and we are far from land. We must try to do what we can: no man can do more."

"Lerntowski said it'd only be a few more days until the governments cave in and S.K.U.N.K. can do what they like. We'll never get to Iceland now in time to stop them. What do you think will happen?" Aisling asked.

"I don't know," Seamus said sombrely. "And I hope we don't find out."

They worked all night (fortunately they were so far north now that it never grew completely dark), and all the next day, hauling the broken mast on board and removing the heavy sail, the yard-arm and the tangled mass of cordage.

The wind was rising and the sea getting rougher. More and more regularly, a wave would crash through the gap in the *Fafnir*'s side. As soon as the mast was clear of it, Thorwald and Archie rigged up a patch with tarpaulin, but the water still came in and Aisling was kept busy taking her turn at the old-fashioned hand pump or helping to bail with pots and pans. Florence plied them continuously with mugs of hot soup and plates of food, but Aisling was too tired to eat. She was cold and wet and miserable and all she wanted to do, she thought as she bailed more water out of the ship, was crawl into her bunk and never wake up again. *Schoolgirl heroine in intrepid crew of Viking ship*! Who was it had told her that sailing was fun? Then another thought struck her. She stopped bailing and went over to Seamus's bed. "Why don't we send out a Mayday message and get help?"

Seamus looked scornfully at her. "Two very good reasons. One: S.K.U.N.K. thinks we're all dead and I prefer to let them continue to think so. And two: we haven't got a radio. Olga was careful to throw both Thorwald's and her own overboard while you were playing detectives on the *Arachne*."

"Oh." Feeling even more cold and wet and miserable, Aisling returned to her bailing. She watched the others working at the mast. She didn't see how they were ever going to mend it. And meanwhile the *Fafnir* was being tossed around in this cold black deserted ocean like a plastic boat in the bath. She remembered a line from a poem they'd done at school, Coleridge's "Ancient Mariner": "Alone, alone, all, all, alone/ alone on a wide wide sea." They would die here. She knew it. Even Florence's vast amount of food would run out in time. And maybe, years from now, someone would come across the drifting ship. *Corpse of schoolgirl found in mysterious Viking ship.* Why hadn't Seamus taken John Smith's advice and stayed at home?

Suddenly Erik gave a shout. "A sail!" he yelled. "It's coming this way!"

Everybody dropped what they were doing and rushed to the side. Sure enough, a sailing ship was bobbing up and down in the crests and troughs of the waves, and it was definitely getting nearer. Aisling's spirits rose. She felt like the people in a wagon trail surrounded by hostile Indians in an old Western film, when the cavalry suddenly gallops up over the horizon to rescue them.

The yacht came nearer. There seemed to be only one person on board.

"Do you think it's someone else from S.K.U.N.K.?" Erik asked.

Aisling looked at the yacht in horror. Had the cavalry suddenly turned into another band of tomahawk-waving Indians? But S.K.U.N.K. thought they were dead. Surely it must be someone else.

She found she was holding her breath as the yacht approached the *Fafnir*. The figure at the tiller became clearer—someone big, wearing bright yellow oilskins. The stranger raised a hand to give a cheery wave. "Ahoy there, *Fafnir*!" The voice, though faint, was vaguely familiar. "Anyone at home?"

Aisling let out her breath. She realized, as she heard herself, what people meant when they talked about a sigh of relief.

Florence patted her curls into place. "There you are. I knew he would come when we needed him. You can always depend on Mr Smith."

"Rubbish, woman," Seamus snorted. "How could he know we were in trouble? It's just pure coincidence that good-for-nothing bookseller is sailing about up here. Trust him to be enjoying a boating holiday when the world is about to be blown apart at any moment."

Aisling thought this was a bit unfair. After all, John Smith had been in Shetland and was obviously deeply involved in whatever the world powers were trying to do to stop S.K.U.N.K. If he was sailing near the magnetic barrier now, he must have been intending to try to get through on his own. And whatever his reason for being here, she thought, she for one was delighted to see him.

So was Mulligan when he climbed aboard. He jumped up onto John Smith's shoulder and rubbed himself against his left ear, purring like a washing machine in spin.

"Get off, you great orange monstrosity! You'll tear my oilskins—though that's about as bad a misnomer as you can get." He looked down smugly at his yellow jacket and trousers. "I very much doubt if these splendid garments have a great deal to do with that glutinous by-product of the rotting of our primaeval forests and swamps into carbon—and I'm pretty sure no poor unfortunate animal's been rendered naked by their manufacture. It's funny how you never think of these things—I wonder just what they *are* made of? You don't happen to have an encyclopedia on board, do you, Grandad?"

"No," Seamus grunted. "Nor a copy of the complete works of Shakespeare."

"A pity, that. No ship should be without a good set of reference books. Nor Shakespeare either, for that matter. There's nothing like a good read on a pleasure cruise."

"If it's a pleasure cruise you're looking for, you've come to the wrong place," Seamus said, looking sourly at the wreckage.

"Ah. That would explain it. I was thinking your ship was in a bit of a mess, but I thought it might be tactless to mention it. Correct me if I'm wrong, but shouldn't the mast be perpendicular rather than horizontal? Or is that the fashion on Viking ships?"

"Not exactly, my friend." Thorwald stepped forward and held out his hand. "I am Thorwald Thorwaldson, captain of the *Fafnir*. Welcome aboard."

"My pleasure." John Smith shook the outstretched hand. "Delighted to meet you all," he beamed as Thorwald introduced him to the rest of the crew. "And it's especially delightful to see dear Florence... Where is Florence, by the way? I was sure I saw her as I came on deck. Where was I? Ah yes, dear Florence, wherever she is, and Seamus, as extrovert (I warned you you should always have an encyclopedia with you, Aisling) and light-hearted as ever."

Fortunately, before Seamus had time to reply, Florence came up on deck again. She had disappeared into the cabin while Thorwald was making the introductions. Now she reappeared carrying a tray covered in a lace tray-cloth and set with delicate china cups and plates, silver cake forks and startlingly white napkins. A gold-rimmed plate with slices of fruit cake on a lace doily completed it. Florence herself was wearing a clean pink pinny with exquisitely embroidered white lace frills.

"Well," she said defensively. "What are you all staring at? A nice cup of tea will do us all good."

"Ye're a great wumman, Florence. I've said it afore and I'll say it again," said Archie warmly. He took the tray from her. "Tak a seat noo, and we'll all hae a cup. The mast can wait a wee moment, after a'."

Aisling couldn't help grinning as she sat down with the others on the cluttered deck. Archie looked like a performing bear, holding the dainty tray in front of him in his huge work-battered hands. And he was gazing at Florence in much the same way as Chris used to gaze at Olga. Chris had been bad enough, she though, but Archie must be over fifty at least! Talk about shipboard romances! There was no way she would drool over anyone like that—ever.

She fed Mulligan a piece of fruit cake and stroked him absently as she listened to the others making plans for repairing the *Fafnir*. Archie and Chris thought that they could cannibalise the mast from John Smith's yacht and use it to replace their own broken one. Thorwald was less optimistic, but agreed to try: "It is better to roof your house with bare branches than to leave it open to the rain and the snow. Beggars cannot be choosers. Our own mast is, I fear, unmendable and any alternative is better than none."

To the surprise of everyone (except Chris and Archie) it worked. Aisling felt her spirits lifting as, after hours of back-breaking work, they raised the yard-arm on the new mast. The great red and white sail, still dripping water, rose slowly up. The new mast bent slightly, but bore the weight. The wind caught in the sail and they started to move northwards again, abandoning John Smith's boat.

"At last," Seamus grunted. "I was beginning to think we'd be there for ever. I just hope we reach Iceland in time. I take it your friends in NATO and in the Warsaw Pact haven't managed to get through the barrier yet?"

"No. Although S.K.U.N.K. must lift it from time to time to get their own men in and out, we've never managed to find out just where and when it's possible to get through. That's why I decided to come up and find you lot. I thought maybe Seamus would succeed where everyone else had failed."

"You sure did do a great job in accessing us here, bud," Otis said warmly. "I didn't think you were going to make it, rendez-vous-wise, at all."

"You mean you *knew* he was going to meet us?" Aisling demanded.

"Sure. We've been in an ongoing communicative situation since we left port. Hadn't you noticed?"

Aisling looked at Erik.

"The submarine?" he suggested.

"Sure." Otis smiled at them. "Though I lost touch with it some days ago and was beginning to wonder if we were heading to engage in a completely different scenario. Especially when the gentlemen from S.K.U.N.K. arrived."

"Aha!" John Smith nodded wisely. "That explains it. I didn't think even Aisling's incompetent sailing could have caused quite this much havoc."

"Of all the cheek!" Aisling glared at him.

"And to think I was quite pleased to see you. Why didn't you stay at home?"

"And miss all the fun? No way, as I think the expression you young things use nowadays goes. Unfortunately I can't check that as I've left my dictionary of modern slang on the boat we've just abandoned. How very careless."

"Rats," Aisling said and went below to help Florence with the supper.

The new mast held and every day brought them nearer and nearer to Iceland. It was never properly dark now, even at midnight, and whales and dolphins appeared in greater and greater numbers. One night, when the sea was covered by a shifting green glow of phosphorescence, a whole school of fin whales passed the *Fafnir*, the phosphorescence glowing eerily on their backs as they rose and fell among the sparkling waves. And once a killer whale came so close that Aisling could see its huge white teeth. As it dived under the ship, she remembered Archie telling them of killer whales, wolves of the sea as the fishermen used to call them, diving under whaling ships and tipping them right over. She didn't dare breathe until its streamlined black-and-white body surfaced again, miles away, on the other side.

They passed through the magnetic shield at 8.43 one morning. Thorwald had been expecting it as the compass had been acting strangely for some time.

"Can we manage without a compass?" Aisling asked anxiously.

"Of course. How do you think the Vikings, or your own St Brendan the Navigator, managed? We use a sextant and the sun—and the North Star at night."

"I have a feeling that, once we're through the barrier, everything will go back to normal," Seamus suggested. "It's the only way that makes sense."

They were eating their breakfast on deck when it happened. Suddenly, the cutlery started to jump about. A knife flew off Aisling's plate and landed on Mulligan's tail. He yelped, turned to spit at her, and streaked into the cabin. The ship shuddered as if a strong breeze had shaken it, but there was no wind. And then, everything was back to normal again. Aisling looked ahead, past the fierce proud head of the dragon bowsprit, towards the horizon. A tall pillar of cloud rose thousands of feet into the air.

"Yon's Iceland, underneath a' that," Archie told her. "It'll no be long now, lass."

"Thank God for that," muttered Seamus. "There is nothing more boring than a long sea trip."

"'I thought only the boring were bored?" Aisling quoted one of his own favourite sayings back at him with great satisfaction.

"Hmph." Seamus refused to be roused. "Pass me that large-scale map of Iceland there and leave me in peace. I imagine they'll be expecting anyone who does get through their precious barrier to head for Reykjavik, so we'll go straight to Snaefellsness and hope to take them by surprise."

"Do you think they know we're still alive, then?" Aisling asked worriedly. "Do they know we're coming?"

"And will they have baked a cake?" John Smith chimed in, mimicking her.

"It's not funny. You weren't there when Shavitov and Lerntowski took over the *Fafnir*, but you know what they're like. I don't want to run into them ever again."

"We should have them in a surprise-situation situation, Aisling. I wouldn't be too worried," Otis reassured her.

Thorwald smiled. "Be patient, Aisling. And do not run to meet troubles. No man knows if he is destined to succeed or to fail. We can but do our best."

Aisling tried to smile back. But with her imagination writing up headlines like *Massacre in Iceland! Crew of Viking ship wiped out*! it wasn't easy.

Thorwald and Seamus spent a long time studying the map of the peninsula called Snaefellsness which lay to the north of Reykjavik on the west coast of Iceland. Snaefellsness was the place Frankie had thought the seismic movement had started, Aisling remembered.

Then Thorwald ordered the sail to be furled and they drifted gently all day. The crew fished, talked and tried to carry on as normal, but everyone was tense, wondering what the night had in store. Although they were still out of sight of land, the ship was surrounded once again by seagulls, much to Mulligan's disgust. He almost managed to catch one which had been stupid enough to land on desk, but it escaped, screaming angrily, after a hectic chase across the foredeck. Mulligan was left with a mouthful of feathers.

When he saw Aisling looking at him, he licked them carefully, as if they were what he'd been after all along.

Thorwald had been hoping for a cloudy night, but the sky was as bright as daylight as he looked at the far northern horizon below which the sun had slipped. "We must do what we have to do," he said. "Fate will decide the outcome. The weather is set fair—we cannot wait for a change. We shall go in tonight."

"I agree," said Seamus.

Aisling picked Mulligan up and held him tightly. She could feel her heart thumping against his orange tummy. He gave her a reproachful look, wriggled out of her arms and jumped onto Seamus's bed.

"Come below with me, child," suggested Florence. "You can help me with some little jobs that need doing."

She got more and more frustrated as each time she finished one of Florence's "little jobs" and tried to go up on deck, Florence found another one for her. But finally, the stores were rearranged, the cabin was spotless and not even Florence could find anything left to do. "All right, child," she said. "Up you go now. Only be quiet and walk softly."

Aisling went up on deck. She blinked. Looming over them, directly ahead of her, was a high black cliff. Behind it, the snow-capped peak of a mountain gleamed in the Arctic twilight.

They had arrived in Iceland!

16
Iceland

lowly they rounded the headland. A bay appeared, sheltered in the arms of cradling cliffs. At its head, a tiny village of little box-like houses nestled around a small jetty. To one side, a wooden church raised its brown spire against the dirty white of a distant glacier.

Silently, the dragon ship glided in towards the pier. The sea was a still blue looking glass, mirroring the mountains and the sky. There was hardly a breath of wind. The houses stared at them with shuttered faces. The only sound was the faint slapping of waves against the prow. Aisling thought that it was as if the whole world was waiting for something to happen.

The *Fafnir* dropped anchor. Aisling looked

anxiously around: would Shavitov suddenly appear from one of the houses? Was Lerntowski hidden somewhere, perhaps in the church belfry, spying on them? She shivered.

She watched anxiously as Thorwald and Chris rowed ashore in the dinghy. It had been decided that, if they managed to land safely without alerting S.K.U.N.K., Thorwald would find the nearest telephone and contact Seamus's friend Hansie in the Icelandic police.

As the Norwegian's tall form disappeared behind the church, Aisling looked round the bay again: still nothing moved. Her skin prickled as if unseen eyes were watching them.

Everyone seemed to feel the same. They spoke in whispers and practically tiptoed round the deck. Even John Smith was silent. Only Florence and Seamus appeared unaffected: Seamus sat up in bed, his Norwegian woolly hat at a jaunty angle, and sketched the scene in front of him, whistling silently through his teeth, while Florence busied herself cooking breakfast.

Chris had stayed in the dinghy, ready to make a quick escape back to the *Fafnir* if necessary. But Thorwald didn't return. Florence came on deck with a tray of bacon and eggs and steaming mugs of coffee. Everyone sat where they could keep an eye on the village and helped themselves. Aisling felt that she'd be too nervous to eat but found, to her surprise, that she was as ravenous as Mulligan.

A dog yapped somewhere in the village. She jumped. Then footsteps sounded, coming nearer.

"Raise the anchor," whispered Archie.

Florence calmly cleared the breakfast things and disappeared into the cabin. She returned a moment later with her pink pinny still tied round her and a murderous-looking crossbow in her hand. Aisling looked at Seamus. He had put down his sketch pad and was now holding an ancient shotgun which she remembered having seen in the studio in Dalkey. Why couldn't they have had them ready when they met the *Arachne*?

Seamus, Aisling noticed, was grinning from ear to ear like a little boy who's been given a year's free supply of sweets. She wished she shared his enthusiasm for dangerous situations.

A figure appeared in the shadow of the church. Aisling's stomach churned and she felt her teeth grating together. Then Thorwald came out of the shadows and crossed the jetty towards them.

There was an audible sigh as everyone let out their breath.

"Hansie is coming," Thorwald reported, as soon as he and Chris were back on board the *Fafnir*.

"I should hope so. You took long enough. These idiots here thought you'd gone and got yourself caught."

"Telephones do not grow on trees, my friend. And," Thorwald smiled, "even if they did, that would be of little help here."

Aisling looked at the bleak treeless hills beyond the village and saw what he meant.

"Well?" Seamus glared at Thorwald impatiently. "What time will he be here? Is he bringing reinforcements? What does he know about S.K.U.N.K.?"

"Very little. It was news to him that S.K.U.N.K. was the reason they were cut off from the rest of the world. You realize, no news has come in for many weeks now. Without knowledge, not even the Arctic fox can hunt his prey. You did not tell me, old friend, that he was the Chief of Police."

"It must have slipped my mind."

"He asked us to anchor at the mouth of the bay. He will come by coastguard launch. It is better so, he says."

"Good." Seamus smiled. "He's a sound man, is Hansie. And we're going to need all the help we can get."

The sun rose higher and the sky turned the pale clear blue which heralds a fine summer's day. The village came to life: smoke trickled from chimney pots, doors opened, people appeared. Someone noticed the Viking ship, still impressive although its sail was furled, riding at anchor at the mouth of the bay. Soon a crowd of people had formed, staring out to sea. The sound of their voices travelled over the still water.

"What are they saying?" Aisling asked Thorwald.

"They are wondering who we are. They are thinking of coming out to see."

"Is that a good idea?"

Thorwald shrugged. "If they have decided to come, we cannot stop them."

A dinghy pulled away from the pier. At the same time, a distant rumble which Aisling had been vaguely aware of to the south turned into the roar of a fast motor boat, causing guillemots and gulls to fly, shrieking, from the cliffs. And then a low black boat screamed round the corner of the bay, spume flying as it cut through the water, and headed straight towards them. Five men were in it, in the uniform of the Icelandic police.

Erik threw a line to the motor boat and four of the men climbed aboard.

Thorwald stepped forward, hand out-stretched, to greet them. The leader hesitated. He was elderly and looked ill and very tired. One of his officers whispered something to him. He drew in his breath and nodded. He grasped Thorwald's hand and squeezed it tightly. Thorwald looked at him in surprise.

"Hansie!" Seamus shouted from the bed. "It's good to see you again! Come over here and tell me what you're doing about this gang of no-good gangsters you've got holed up in Snaefellsness."

Hansie pressed Thorwald's hand again. As he went aft to speak to Seamus, his men fanned out on the deck. One went to stand beside Florence. He took her crossbow and examined it curiously.

"I doubt ye hinna seen ane o' them afore, laddie," Archie commented. "It's nae an afa' lot o' wummen hae a crossbow in the larder—and know how tae use it as weel. I've said it afore and I'll say it again—you're a great wumman, Florence."

Florence blushed.

Aisling turned to see what Hansie and Seamus were doing. Hansie, looking very grave, was bending down to speak to Seamus. Seamus suddenly went tense. His blue-veined hand stretched out for the shotgun which he'd put down on the duvet beside Mulligan when Thorwald had come back on board.

Before he had time to reach it, one of Hansie's men kicked it out of the way. He drew a gun and pointed it at Seamus.

The other policemen also drew their pistols.

I don't believe it, Aisling thought. They can't have caught us twice with the same trick. Rats, double rats and more rats!

John Smith was standing beside her. He smiled. "Here we go again, eh? It's amazing the lack of imagination they have. If I'd known, I could have brought them a book I have back at the shop: *Ninety-six ways to Take Your Enemy by Surprise*. If we're going to be caught napping, it'd be nice if they changed their tactics now and again. Variety is, as they say, the spice of life."

"Shut up!" a policeman snarled at him.

"Why?" John Smith asked. "Don't you have an Auntie Mary? Mine always told me that conversation oils the wheels of social intercourse. As all of you are just standing around dumbly, I thought you were waiting for one of us to start the ball rolling."

The policeman raised his pistol.

A command rang out in a foreign language. Aisling recognised the high squeaky voice. She turned round. Sure enough, Lerntowski was coming aboard and behind him, puffing like an unfit walrus, was Shavitov.

Quadruple rats, she thought. "Mulligan!" she hissed, as loudly as she dared. "Here, Mulligan! Food!"

But Mulligan, after growling in disgust at having been wakened by inconsiderate people messing with shotguns while he was trying to rest, had put his nose back down on his paws and was fast asleep again.

"So," squeaked Lerntowski. "We meet again. You lead a charmed life, old man."

"Not charmed enough," growled Seamus. "It's continuously being spoilt by you and your ugly minions interfering in it."

Lerntowski scowled. "We will have to teach you manners, Grandaddy. I have had enough of your insults. This time, I shall deal with you personally." He spat out an order to his men.

"No way," said Seamus. "I am staying in this bed."

"So? You understand our language?"

Seamus didn't bother answering.

Shavitov lumbered forwards, his arms outstretched.

"No." Lerntowski stopped him. He looked thoughtfully from Seamus to the crowd in the village, all avidly watching the two boats. Aisling followed his gaze. Of course: why hadn't she thought of it before? The curious onlookers must be wondering what was going on. She looked for the dinghy which had been coming out to meet them: it must have decided it didn't want to tangle with what it thought was a police launch and had returned to shore. But the morning was so still the people there would definitely hear her if she shouted for help. She opened her mouth.

Before she could get the first word out, Shavitov clamped his huge hand over her face and twisted her head backwards. She bit as hard as she could. His grip tightened until she could hardly breathe.

"So? You zeenk you can make troubles for us again, no? You zeenk you can, how you say? put ze screwdriver in ze vodka? Zees time, ve show you ve are not to be trifled viz. Zees time, ve keel you very, very slow."

Lerntowski smiled at him—a smile that

made Aisling's blood run cold. "You deserve your fun, my friend. But not in front of the good Icelandic people there. They might begin to think we are not the noble police force we pretend to be." He switched back to the foreign language. Aisling listened, but couldn't make out a word he said. She wondered how much Seamus really understood.

Then Lerntowski spoke in English again. "You," he said to Aisling, "and the boy, can go with Shavitov here. He is good at keeping little children amused." He looked round the others and saw John Smith. His eyes went cold. "So you are here, too. You double-crossed me before. You shall not do so again. I think I will allow my large friend to have his fun with you too. And, perhaps, the brave lady with the crossbow. She should learn that a woman's place is in the home, not interfering with the work of men."

"I'm staying with Seamus," Florence said calmly. "He needs me."

Lerntowski shrugged. "He will not need you long. But I shall not argue with you. The old seaman and the red-haired one I shall bring with us: I may have a use for you. And I think Grandaddy should be allowed to watch the final destruction—it should appeal to his stubborn nature. So, come. Let us get out of here. Take the children and our knowledgeable friend into the launch."

Aisling, Erik and John Smith were hustled into the launch. Chris, to Aisling's surprise, came with them and, to her even greater surprise, nobody stopped him.

As she was climbing down the ladder, Florence came over with Seamus's rug in her arms. She handed it to John Smith. "Don't let Aisling get cold, Mr Smith. And make sure she eats properly. With her parents not here, I feel responsible for her. I don't know what they would say if they knew what she was up to."

Aisling couldn't imagine either. She wondered if anyone would ever know what had happened to her. They'd phone Mrs Ruttledge soon anyway, wondering why she hadn't come home. And then the fat would truly be in the fire. *Irish schoolgirl last seen disappearing over horizon on Viking ship.* And, she grinned wryly, if she did ever get home again, they'd absolutely kill her for all the worry she'd caused.

Shavitov saw her smile. "You are happy leetle girl, yes? You vill not be so for long. I, Shavitov, promise you zees."

One of the fake policemen on the launch

threw a line to the *Fafnir* and they started to tow the Viking ship out of the bay. The crowd on the shore watched them go.

Aisling thought of making a last desperate appeal for help, but it was impossible: the four of them had been herded into the middle of the launch and were being guarded by another fake policeman with a gun. There was no way any of them could do anything but stand there, waiting to see what S.K.U.N.K. would do next.

17
Captured Again

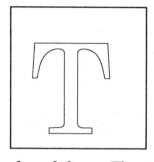hey didn't have long to wait. About twenty minutes later, the launch slowed down. The tow-rope to the *Fafnir* was cast off and then the launch roared on. Aisling watched as the expanse of water between the two ships lengthened—would she ever see Seamus and Florence again? She was so sunk in misery that she hardly noticed when the launch's engine slowed again and they turned into another small bay. She let herself be pushed ashore with the others and herded into a wooden shed next to a tumbledown hut.

"I, Shavitov, vill hav my lunch. You vill, how you say?...stew here and zink about vat Shavitov vill do viz you. Vat ees eet ze Americans say? See you, yes? I vill see you later, my friends."

He shut the door and left them in darkness. They heard the launch move off.

John Smith peered through a crack at the side of the door. "The launch is picking up the *Fafnir* again. I wonder where it's taking Seamus and Florence."

Aisling had been wondering something else. Shavitov's mention of Americans had reminded her of Otis. "Where's Otis?" she asked.

"On the *Fafnir*," said Erik.

"Are you sure?" Chris asked. "I didn't see him there after S.K.U.N.K. arrived. Did you?"

"No. Come to think of it, I didn't."

Nor had John Smith seen him either.

"That proves it!" Aisling was triumphant. "He's a S.K.U.N.K. agent after all! None of you would believe me."

"Are you sure?" Chris repeated. "Why did he stay on the *Fafnir* when they tricked us before, then? He didn't know Shavitov wasn't throwing petrol around."

"Oh. Unless..." Aisling thought quickly. "It could have been all a double-bluff. Maybe Shavitov never intended to use petrol." She looked at John Smith. "If they knew you were coming to help us, they might have planned it all..."

John Smith smiled at her confusion.

"Exactly. They might indeed. Though perhaps your explanation does somewhat overreach the bounds of verisimilitude (from the Latin *veritas*, truth, and *similitudo*, a likeness, as any good dictionary would tell you). Although I grant you that sightings of red herrings are not completely unheard of either."

Erik looked blank. Aisling sulked.

"I must say that makes me feel better," Chris said. "I mean that Otis has escaped. I hope he manages to rescue us soon."

"How will he find us?" Erik asked.

"If he'd followed the ship, he'd have seen where the launch left us."

"Not unless he had transport," said John Smith. "And you must also ask yourselves the question, my optimistic young friends: would he want to find us?"

"So you do think he's a spy!"

"Don't be so paranoid, Aisling." Chris turned to John Smith. "What do you mean? Of course he'd want to find us. He can't tackle S.K.U.N.K. alone. And, anyway, he wouldn't leave us for Shavitov...would he?"

"He would, if he thought the cause of the US of A would profit by it. Remember, our American friends have only one plan: they intend to nuke this island out of existence, thus nuking S.K.U.N.K. into the wide blue yonder also. If Otis can infiltrate their headquarters and lift the barrier: bingo! as my dear Aunt Mary, bless her full houses and ninety-nines, used to say."

"Oh." Aisling's spirits hit rock bottom again. She suddenly felt dead tired. She sat down on the floor and put her head on her knees.

A wet furry nose poked into her cheek.

She sat up abruptly. "Mulligan! How did you get here?"

Mulligan gave her a few licks with his sandpapery tongue and flopped down across her lap.

"Thank Florence's solicitude. An interesting word, that, Aisling. A typical example of a change in usage over the years: it originally meant anxiety for one's self; but now, much more altruistically, means anxiety for others."

Aisling decided not to ask what altruistically meant.

"She wrapped him in the rug," Erik explained. "It was very clever of her. Perhaps we can use him to save us from Shavitov again."

Aisling hugged Mulligan tightly as she thought of Shavitov coming to get them. "I wonder how long he'll take to finish his dinner?"

she asked worriedly.

"Long enough, I should think, if his size is any reflection on his appetite. I suggest we see if we can get out of here before he comes back. Unless you would prefer to continue this fascinating conversation? We could, for example, go on to discuss the price of cheese?"

Chris and Erik felt their way round the inside walls of the shed. It was very solidly built.

"There's only the crack by the door," Erik said. "And there's a guard just outside. There's no way we could force the door open without his hearing us."

Chris agreed with him. "I was hoping there'd be some rotten timbers. But these Icelanders build too well—this place is as solid as a whiskey barrel. Damn it."

"Can you see anyone else?" John Smith asked. "Any other guards?"

Erik peered through the crack again. "No. But I suppose there could be someone round the other side or in the house with Shavitov or whatever he's called."

"Only the two of them came off the boat with us," Aisling pointed out.

"True, o child of incredible perspicacity (from the Latin *perspicax*, *perspicacem*, having the power of seeing through). But there could have been someone here already."

"Why do you always have to point out these things?" Aisling asked irritably.

"It's my bright and positive nature." He smiled at her. "Let us not despair. In the hour of need, a man may discover his wit is sharpened, as your father, Erik, might have said."

"I've an idea," Chris said suddenly. "Start groaning, Ash. Pretend you're really badly hurt."

Aisling looked at him suspiciously. "Why?"

"Good idea," Erik backed up Chris. "If they think you're hurt, they'll come in and then we can thump them over the head and get away."

"Do we have to take our plans from the *Boys' Own Book of Adventure Stories*?" John Smith groaned. "Still, it might work. I doubt if our friend Fatso is a great reader and he may never have heard of it. He's also thick enough to fall for it. Apart from which, I can't come up with anything better. Also..." He chuckled. "We do have a secret weapon."

"Sorry?"

"Mulligan. If Fatso comes in we throw the moggy at him and—ta-ra!—he sneezes fit to blow the roof off. Which might come in handy too."

"You can't hurt Mulligan!"

"Sorry, Aisling. But we have to get out of here. Apart from the pleasant little party Shavitov's dreaming up for us, I don't like the idea of all our Golden Oldies being towed away by S.K.U.N.K. Nor do I particularly savour the thought of our American cousin beavering away on his own to bring the bombers in. Apart from which, Mulligan can look after himself, if any cat can."

"Okay, now. Chris, see if you can find something heavy and take one side of the door. I'll take the other. Erik, you hold Mulligan and be ready to throw him. All right? Now, Aisling. Start groaning!"

Aisling moaned feebly.

"Louder, girl. You're supposed to be at death's door, not worrying about your hairdo."

Aisling glared at him. Unfortunately, he couldn't see her in the dark. She imagined she was dying. Her mother and father and Kevin were all gathered round the bed, looking down at her anxiously. She groaned miserably.

"That's better. A bit louder still."

Aisling thought of being locked up with John Smith and an encyclopedia for ever and groaned as loudly as she could.

John Smith rapped on the door. "Hey! You out there! We need help. The girl's dying."

There was no answer.

He started to kick the door so that it shook on its hinges. The whole shed vibrated.

"Stop!" The guard sounded alarmed.

"The girl needs help. Girl! Sick! Fetch boss! Shavitov! God give me patience! Why do I have to deal with a moron that doesn't even speak English? How on earth is one supposed to mislead someone when they don't even know they're being led in the first place?" John Smith sighed and tried again: "Fetch boss! Quick! Chop, chop!"

"That's pidgin English," Chris pointed out. "You can't expect him to speak like a nineteenth-century Chinaman."

"I don't expect him to speak like anything. I expect him to listen and act on it. Keep up the moaning, Aisling."

Aisling continued to groan theatrically.

Chris put an eye to the crack in the door. "It's worked. He's gone over to the house. Should we try breaking the door down?"

"Wait till he gets inside."

"Damn. He's stopped. He's shouting something. Now he's turned and his machine gun's pointed this way again."

"Uhuh." John Smith kicked at the door again. "She's getting worse!" he yelled.

"Monster Man's coming," Chris reported. "He doesn't look pleased. We've interrupted his lunch—there's half a loaf of bread in his greasy paw."

"Okay. Ready all of you?"

"What about the guard? He's coming too."

"Play it by ear. If Fatso comes in first, let him get right into the room. You stay by the door. When Erik chucks the moggy, zonk the guard with whatever you've found there. Okay? And keep groaning, Aisling. Don't stop now."

Aisling groaned heartbreakingly. *Irish schoolgirl chosen as heroine in moving new film...*

"Good girl," John Smith whispered. "Keep it up."

Shavitov's voice came from the far side of the door. "Vat ees zees? You are fooling me, yes?"

"No," shouted John Smith. "The girl is sick."

"So? You zink I should care, yes? Ees very naughty girl. Eet has insulted me, Shavitov, many times. Eet has bittet me. And you zink I should vorry eef eet dies?"

"I thought you wanted to, what did you say?...play with us first. You can't do that if she's dead," John Smith pointed out reasonably.

Aisling moaned louder than ever. With Shavitov right outside the door, it wasn't difficult to sound desperate.

"All right. I come to see. But eef zere ees any funny business, I see zat you suffer, yes?"

The key groaned in the lock, bolts were drawn and the door opened. "Vere ees she?"

"Over here. She can't get up. I tell you, she's dying."

Shavitov snapped something at the guard who positioned himself at the doorway, his machine gun at the ready.

Shavitov stepped towards Aisling.

All hell broke loose.

Erik, who had been standing in the shadows with Mulligan in his arms, suddenly threw him at Shavitov. Jerked out of the half-doze he'd fallen into and caught off-balance, Mulligan put his claws out and clung to the object he'd landed on: Shavitov's head. The head moved violently. Mulligan hung on even more tightly, scrabbling for a foothold on Shavitov's face with his back paws, claws extended. He yowled and spat viciously to show just what he thought of such treatment.

Shavitov tore at the cat, trying to remove him. The others watched, stunned. Then Chris came to his senses, raised the crowbar he'd found as a weapon, and, just as the guard let loose a burst of machine-gun fire, crashed it down over his head. Bullets ricocheted around the corrugated iron roof and the guard collapsed, unconscious.

Erik grabbed the machine gun and pointed it at Shavitov. "Put your hands up," he yelled.

Shavitov was still struggling with Mulligan. He had started sneezing now, and was floundering about the shed like an elephant with hay fever trying to brush off a swarm of tsetse flies.

"Excuse me." John Smith took the crowbar from Chris and swung it at Shavitov's legs, bringing him crashing to the ground. Mulligan leapt off and fled, spitting and growling, to the far corner of the shed. John Smith used the crowbar again and knocked Shavitov out. "Just doing him a favour, really, poor man," he remarked, putting down the bar and wiping his fingers on his sweater. "He really should get that allergy seen to some day." He looked down at the two unconscious men. "There we are then, folks. I suggest we let them sleep in peace. Aisling, corral that cat (check it up in a dictionary of Wild Western slang) and let's get out of here."

18

The Radar Station

isling grabbed Mulligan and followed the others out of the shed. John Smith locked and bolted the door. "I doubt if either of our sleeping beauties will wake up in the next hour or so, but, just in case Prince Charming comes along to give them the kiss of life, we'd better take the key with us."

"I wonder where Lerntowski is," Aisling said. "Do you think he'll come here?" She looked round the quiet cove and shivered.

"He's no reason to at the moment. And, when he does, we'll be long gone. But first, let's have a look at the hut. It might give us a clue as to where we'll find S.K.U.N.K."

The hut looked as if it had been deserted for a long time. There was a smell of dirt and mice, dust lay over everything, the curtains were ripped, the panelling of the walls had been torn out to use as firewood. In the main room someone, Shavitov presumably, had lit a fire. A camping stove stood on the table and a pan of glutinous stew was still simmering on it.

Mulligan rushed towards the table, his tail up, his nose twitching. Chris poured some of the stew onto a dirty plate and placed it on the floor. Mulligan dived at it, then jumped back with a yelp as he burnt his tongue.

"Serves you right for being so greedy," said John Smith. He broke a piece of the loaf which was lying on the table and dunked it in the remainder of the stew. "Not exactly *haute cuisine*, but not as bad as it looks. I suggest we follow Mulligan's example and have a snack. Waste not, want not, as the poet has it."

"What poet?" Aisling asked coldly.

"Some poet or other. You'll always find a poet if you look hard enough: as another one said, the fellow who wrote the Book of Ecclesiastes in the Bible, if my memory serves me right, 'there is no new thing under the sun'."

"Big deal."

"Come on, Aisling. Stop arguing with him. You know he always wins." Erik offered her a piece of bread. "This stew is really not too bad.

As the old saying goes: eat when you can, for who knows where the next meal is coming from."

"Thanks," said Aisling. "That really cheers me up." She took the bread and ate her share of the stew all the same.

John Smith searched the room. All he found was a lurid picture love story, a few packets of biscuits and some chocolate bars. He shared the latter out. "Erik's right. Put these in your pockets and keep them for an emergency."

"What about the book?" Chris asked with a grin. "Who takes it?"

John Smith held it between his finger and thumb and looked at it in disgust. "I knew our fat friend wasn't exactly the Creator's most successful attempt at an intelligent life form, but I didn't think he sank as low as this. I don't normally hold with book burning—it's the first sign of the end of civilisation as we may or may not know it; but I think we'll consign this garbage to the flames. I'd hate to corrupt a poor passing peasant."

He threw the book on the fire.

"There might have been a clue in that," Aisling pointed out. "It could have been in code or something."

"And pigs could travel aerodynamically."

"Can we go? " Chris asked patiently. "If we stay here much longer, that pair of heavies in the shed will wake up and wonder why we're still around. I'm beginning to wonder myself."

"Right. Lead on, Macduff." John Smith put an arm round Aisling and led her out through the door. "Though it actually reads 'lay on Macduff' in *Macbeth*, as I'm sure you'd want to know," he whispered conspiratorially.

She ducked out from under his arm. "Get lost," she suggested.

They found a dinghy with an outboard motor moored under the jetty. They climbed in, Erik started the motor, shattering the calm of the little bay, and they roared out to sea. Looking back, Aisling thought she saw the shed shaking, but she couldn't be sure. With any luck, Shavitov and his assistant would stay trapped until they'd finished in Iceland and were safely on their way back to Dublin. Though with Seamus and the others captured, and none of them having the slightest idea where S.K.U.N.K. were operating from, that could be long enough, she thought gloomily.

"North or south?" Erik asked as they reached open sea.

"Did anyone see which way they towed the *Fafnir*?"

"No. You couldn't see much through that crack."

"Hmm." John Smith looked up and down the coast thoughtfully. "The village we were at before must be round that headland there. And the police launch that wasn't came from this direction. So, either they started from our cove here, or they came from further north. I vote we go north and have a look. There's a radio mast sticking up along the coast up there. Can you see it? It might be worth looking into."

"Okay," said Erik and turned the boat round. "You're the boss."

"Is he?" Aisling asked. "Why?"

"He's been trained by MI5, Aisling," Chris told her. "He knows what to do."

"I'm glad somebody does." Aisling wondered why she felt so grumpy. She picked up Mulligan and hugged him until he growled with disgust, wriggled out of her arms and settled himself across her knees. It was just that none of the others seemed to be worrying in the slightest about what was going to happen to them— while she, she admitted to herself as she stroked Mulligan's glossy fur, was scared stiff. If she hadn't been so pig-headed, she'd be safe at home in Dalkey now, she reminded herself.

It was one thing to dream up exciting headlines about yourself in the papers—quite another sitting in a small boat miles from home and scared to death!

As they got nearer to the radio mast, they were able to see buildings crouched on the cliffs beneath it. On the roof of one of the buildings were what looked like huge metal saucers standing on their edges. "It must be the radar station," Erik said. "There should be one on this coast."

"Good. Maybe they can point us to S.K.U.N.K.'s headquarters. Or at least put us in touch with the police."

"But Hansie's the police and they've got him," Aisling objected.

"I know, oh bright young thing. We shall have to go carefully. I very much doubt, though, that S.K.U.N.K. have managed to get complete control of the whole of the Icelandic police and armed forces, even if they've abducted our friend Hansie by some foul means. There must be a few good men left in Setzuan."

"Where?"

"Sorry. A reference to Bertolt Brecht, the great German playwright. I get carried away, sometimes."

"Do you ever enter for table quizzes?" Chris

asked. "You'd sweep the board."

"Are we going to land or not?" Erik wanted to know. "Or do I keep on going?"

"We'll land. Unless Aisling would prefer to motor up and down the coast until we run out of petrol, in the hope that we pass a huge notice somewhere: *Visit S.K.U.N.K.! See how to split the world in half! Free tours every half hour!*"

"I still think we should try and find them ourselves. That place might belong to them. We'd be walking straight into their arms."

"There are only four of us, Aisling. Going it alone is all very well in Enid Blyton, but getting the authorities to back you up makes a lot of sense in the real world. However, I take your point: we will be careful."

Aisling looked up at the building on the cliff top. If Lerntowski was up there, waiting for them... She felt, not for the first time this voyage, like a character in one of the Asterix books, waiting for the sky to fall in on their heads.

They landed on a shingly beach and pulled the boat beyond the high-water mark. Then they climbed the grassy cliff, amid clumps of sea pinks and white campion bells with here and there the purple spike of an orchid. They had to cross a narrow strip of bog to reach the track which led to the radar station. Huge brown birds and others, smaller and more streamlined but just as vicious, flew at them screaming raucously. Mulligan struggled, growling excitedly, in Aisling's arms, trying to get a swipe at them as they dive-bombed past her, just inches away from her head. She held on to him tightly and hoped they'd reach the road soon. "All skuas are dangerous when they're protecting their nests," Erik explained. "We must be crossing a breeding area."

"You can tell that by the smell." Chris grunted. "Hurry up, you lot. I want to reach civilisation again."

"Civilisation," John Smith sighed, looking ahead to where the road passed through the high metal fence, topped by barbed wire, which surrounded the complex of buildings. "Sometimes I think I prefer nature red in tooth and claw and smelling to high heaven." He dodged to escape an arctic skua seemingly intent on a kamikaze mission. "Although other times, I'm not so sure."

A barrier straddled the road as it passed through the fence, and a building like a sentry box stood beside it. Inside this sat a uniformed man, reading a newspaper. He put it down as they approached.

"Já?"

"And a very good morning to you too, sir. You wouldn't, by any happy chance, speak English, would you? Or is that too much to ask?" John Smith smiled warmly at him.

"Ney," the man grunted. "Íslensku og Dönsku." He gave them a surly look and returned to his newspaper. Aisling wondered if all Icelanders were as rude to strangers— she hoped not.

"He only speaks Icelandic and Danish," Erik explained. He said a few words in what Aisling assumed was Danish. The man scowled, picked up the phone in front of him, pressed a button and said something into it. There was a reply. He put the receiver down and grunted something again.

"He says to wait here."

A jeep moved away from the main building and came down the road towards them. The driver motioned to them to get in. John Smith tried speaking to him in English, Erik in Danish, but he maintained a stony silence. Two down, and one as rude as the other, Aisling thought.

The driver stopped the jeep at the entrance to the main building, got out and motioned

them to follow him. They passed through glass
entrance doors into a wide lobby. It was
deserted. Their guide led them downstairs and
along a corridor. Again, they passed no one.

"It's very quiet," Aisling whispered. "Where
is everyone? I don't like it—I think S.K.U.N.K.
has taken over here."

"Perhaps. And again, perhaps not. They
could be all having a late dinner break. Keep
your eyes open, though."

They turned into another corridor. This one
had windows all along one side through which
they could see a room full of machinery, dials
and flashing lights. Aisling looked through the
glass curiously, wondering what all the
machines were for. To direct planes and boats,
she supposed, if Erik was right and it was a
radar station. There seemed to be an awful lot
of machines.

Then one of the technicians turned to speak
to another. Aisling froze.

It was Olga!

The guide grabbed her arm and pulled her
away. He looked angry. "Follow!" he ordered
abruptly.

Aisling caught up with John Smith. "I was
right!" she whispered urgently. "I've just seen
Olga. This place is being run by S.K.U.N.K.—

we have to get out!"

He looked at her. "Are you sure?"

"Yes."

"Okay. We take evasive action. Can you distract our tall silent friend, there?"

Aisling dropped Mulligan and pretended to trip over him. "Ouch!" she yelped, lying on the floor and holding her ankle.

Chris turned to come back. "Are you all right, Ash?"

"I think I've sprained my ankle. Ouch! I can't get up."

The guard grabbed her roughly by the shoulder. "Up!" he ordered angrily. John Smith was behind him, his hand raised. Aisling just managed to roll aside in time to avoid being squashed by the guard's falling body.

She picked up Mulligan again and stood up. "That was effective," she said.

"All part of the service. You've no idea what they teach you in MI5. Now come on, let's get out of here."

Chris looked bewildered. "What's going on?" he asked.

Aisling hesitated. She didn't want to tell him Olga was here. "I saw a S.K.U.N.K. agent. They've taken the place over. We'll have to be careful when we pass that control room window on the way back."

They crept along close to the floor to avoid being seen by anyone inside the room. Aisling went first, crawling awkwardly with Mulligan held in one hand. It seemed to take ages to reach the bend in the corridor, but she got there at last without anyone from the control room raising the alarm. She was just about to stand up when she saw, in front of her, a pair of brown leather brogues. Her heart seemed to stop beating—and then started up again like a sledgehammer.

"What's up?" whispered Erik, who was behind her.

Aisling got up slowly. She let her breath out in a gasp of relief: it was Otis! Seconds later her heart started to pound again: what if she'd been right before and he was a S.K.U.N.K. agent? They'd know very soon, anyway, if he raised the alarm.

"Otis!" Erik exclaimed. "How did you get here?"

"Before I address that question, perhaps you could tell me what is going on, situation-wise?" Otis suggested.

"No problem, bud," said John Smith who had joined them. "Situation-wise, we're in a getting-out-of-here-pretty-damned-quick situation, before S.K.U.N.K. realizes we are not walking innocently into their loving arms. Come on."

"I believe I'll take a rain check on that: I have business here at this moment in time. That room contains the equipment which controls the magnetic barrier—it is imperative that I expeditiously deactivate the machinery."

"What does that mean?" whispered Erik to John Smith.

"Translated into English, I think it means that he wants to raise the magnetic barrier to let the nuclear bombers in and flatten this cute little island. Would that be correct, assessment-wise? Or have I misread the situation-situation?"

Otis grinned. "You can't make an omelette without breaking eggs, as our good friend Thorwald might have said. Somebody has to make sure the world is kept safe for democracy."

Aisling realized that he must have been speaking the truth when he'd said he was with the CIA. She wondered, with all this talk about bombs, whether she'd have preferred him to be in S.K.U.N.K. after all. They, at least, made no excuses about saving the world for democracy.

"You think these machines back there

operate the barrier?" Chris asked. "I'd love to know how they do it." And before anyone could stop him, he'd gone back round the corner and was peering in through the glass.

"Hey, everybody! It's Olga! Olga's here, safe and sound!" He rapped on the glass. "Olga! It's me, Chris!"

John Smith grabbed his arm and pulled him away. "Come on! You too, Otis—you'll never get in there now!"

Alarm bells were sounding as they rushed back to the entrance hall and out through the door. The jeep was still there. They bundled Chris into it, John Smith took the wheel, and they roared off. "Hold on!" He crashed through the barrier at full speed. They held on tightly as the jeep careered at a breakneck rate down the narrow rutted road.

"We've left Olga behind!" Chris moaned. "Why didn't you wait for her?"

"Will you ever get it into your besotted head that Olga's working for S.K.U.N.K.!"

"If she is, it's only because they have some hold over her. We could have saved her! You've never appreciated her, Aisling. I didn't think you were the jealous type."

"There's someone coming behind us!" Erik shouted.

John Smith pressed the accelerator to the floor and the jeep skidded over the stones on the rough road. "I can't keep this up—we'll overturn."

"They're still there."

"In that case, we'd better take to the sea." He turned off the road and bumped across the bog. If the skuas had been excited before, they were completely maddened now. They wheeled in a swirling cloud overhead, diving down at the jeep and its occupants. The jeep drove into a bog hole and stopped. "Run for it!" shouted John Smith.

Aisling grabbed Mulligan and followed the others back to the spot where they'd come up from the beach. They slithered down the hill and dragged the boat across the shingle to the water's edge.

Aisling looked up. The raucous cloud of skuas were diving at three figures on the cliff top. As Chris pushed the boat clear of the shore and Erik started the motor, a shot whizzed past Aisling's head and splashed into the sea in front of her. She ducked. Another shot followed: *Irish schoolgirl shot dead on remote Icelandic beach*! She hoped they'd be out of range soon.

Erik steered the boat out to sea, zig-zagging

to avoid the bullets. He stopped when they were out of range.

"Now what?" he asked.

"We go back," Otis said. "We have to access that control room and directionalize the boys or we'll all be down the tubes."

"I agree with Otis. We've got to save Olga from these criminals. Whatever Aisling says, I know she's not working for them willingly."

Aisling groaned. "I give up. Remind me never to fall in love."

"Do you think my father is up there?" Erik looked up at the white buildings.

"I don't know." John Smith spoke more seriously than usual. "I haven't forgotten the others and I'm well aware that the sooner we find them, the better. Lerntowski may pretend to be more civilised than Shavitov, but I wouldn't trust him too far either."

"So we're going back there?" Aisling looked at the cliff top in horror.

"I didn't say that. I think we should try to find the *Fafnir*. They can't have brought her here—there's no place they could have hidden her. I suggest we go on back south and find where they've landed her. After all, a Viking ship is pretty obvious. And, wherever she is, that's where we'll find Seamus and the others too."

19
Ten Little Indians

s they travelled south, back past the cove where Shavitov had held them prisoner and where, Aisling hoped fervently, he was still locked up (she stared at the hut as they passed but couldn't see if the door was open or shut), they noticed a black car on the road which ran along the top of the cliffs. It was obviously following them. Then the car suddenly disappeared—the road must have curved inland, she thought with relief.

They rounded a headland of low black cliffs. The surf snarled as it sucked at the rocks; sea birds—guillemots, puffins, fulmars, herring gulls—squawked and screeched, disputing nesting ledges and wheeling on the upcurrents like scraps of paper in the wind.

Aisling gradually became aware of another

noise, behind the pounding of the surf and the screaming of the gulls. "What's that?" she asked.

"What?" Erik eased back the motor.

A black dot appeared in the sky behind them. "A helicopter. I might have guessed." John Smith frowned. "We'd better get in close to these cliffs."

"Isn't that a cave? That blacker bit there?"

"You're right, Aisling, light of my life. Rejoice, for salvation may be at hand."

The cave proved to be wide and deep. Erik cut the engine as soon as they were under the cliff. They waited. They heard the helicopter come nearer and pass overhead.

"It can't have seen us," Aisling whispered.

"Let's hope not. Though, when it finds we've disappeared, it's bound to get suspicious. I'm sure they'll be sending out a boat as well, before too long."

She looked up at the dark cliffs towering above them: the seabirds nesting on the ledges at the cave entrance looked back at her, kak-kak-kaking in alarm. She shivered: if S.K.U.N.K. found them here, they'd have no escape. *Massacre in Icelandic cave!* But would the news ever reach the papers? She doubted it. They could all be murdered here and no-one would be the wiser.

Otis was listening to the fading roar of the helicopter. "Okay, you guys. I believe we have a conflict of interest situation here. Chris and I want to re-access that radar station and the rest of you want to find the *Fafnir*. I suggest we divide our forces, numerically-wise: Chris and I climb up the cliff here and sneak back to the station, while you and the kids address yourselves to the problems of the ship, location-wise. Can you give me your reaction to that suggestion?"

"Good idea, Otis." Chris was enthusiastic.

John Smith frowned. "I don't like the idea of splitting up—we've already lost half our party. And I'd prefer to find the *Fafnir* before it's too late. I still believe that the radar station back there isn't the centre of S.K.U.N.K.'s operations; after all, that mincing moron Lerntowski offered Seamus a ringside view of the final sub-oceanic upheaval, so he must have been taking him to wherever the earthquakes are controlled from. Which was back this way, somewhere. I vote we go on."

"With respect," Otis objected (not very respectfully, Aisling thought), "you might take forever to access the *Fafnir*. We don't have time to hang about playing hunt the thimble.

The bottom line is as follows: if we don't raise that barrier now, timewise, S.K.U.N.K. will split the ocean in two. We have to act."

"I agree with Otis," Erik said slowly. "We're not going to find the *Fafnir*, so the best we can do is to let the bombers in and at least stop S.K.U.N.K. from causing any more harm. The future of the world is more important than my father—or all of us."

"But they'll use nuclear bombs!" Aisling pointed out. "You can't be for that, can you?"

Erik looked at Otis. "You don't need nuclear bombs, do you? Conventional ones will be enough to blow up Snaefellsness, surely—and we know that's where S.K.U.N.K. is operating from."

"I hear what you're saying. And I agree to evaluate the situation on location. But the final decision, bomb-wise, is a higher command prerogative, decision-wise. Now, will you access the base of that cliff, please."

John Smith looked up at the cliff. "Don't be daft, man. You'll never climb that, any-which-wise. Not unless you're Spider-Man, or whatever that malformed, misbegotten character on the box is called."

"It's okay," Chris interrupted calmly. "I've been looking at it."

"And you're an expert on cliff-climbing are you, Christopher?"

"Well, maybe not an expert. But I am leader of the Dalkey Quarry Rock Climbing Club and I do know what I'm talking about."

"Good." Otis smiled. "Come on, then, bud. The sooner we get that control room in an eyeball to eyeball interface situation, the better. Move the boat out a bit till we conceptualize the cliff, Erik, please."

Erik looked from Otis to John Smith.

"Stay where you are," John Smith told him.

Otis raised his trouser leg and removed a knife he had strapped inside his sock. He laid the point of the blade against Erik's neck. "I had hoped it wouldn't be imperative to engage in a confrontational mode of interaction, but I see I have no alternative. Now, move the boat in, please."

Erik looked at John Smith again. He shrugged. "Go ahead, lad. My Aunt Hortensia always told me never to argue with cold steel and she may, for once, have been right."

As the boat approached the foot of the cliffs, Chris examined them carefully. "It doesn't look too bad. Even without ropes. There's plenty of ledges and it's not that high. We'll have to look out for the fulmars, though—they tend to spit at you if you get too close."

"Won't the men in the black car be up there waiting for you?" Aisling asked.

"Not necessarily. They've probably gone further round the coast to check on where we've gotten to, destination-wise."

"You'd better hurry, if you're going," Erik suggested sourly. "There's a band of fog coming up. I wouldn't like to climb a cliff in that."

"Great," Otis said. "That's just what we need, cover-wise. We may even be able to access the car and highjackize it. All right, now—you go first, Chris."

As Erik held the boat steady, Chris waited for a suitable moment and then jumped onto a projecting ledge. Aisling admired his coolness. The thought of climbing a cliff like that sent goose-pimples along her spine. Otis wasn't so lucky—or so competent, perhaps. The boat moved just as he jumped and he fell into the sea. Aisling thought for a moment he was going to be crushed between the boat and the sharp black rocks, but Chris managed to get hold of him and haul him out onto the ledge beside him. Funnily enough, she was glad he'd been saved—even though it might have been better for them if he'd slipped into the sea, knife and all, and died: if he did manage to raise the magnetic barrier and his bosses sent nuclear bombers in, none of them would survive.

"I told you he was rotten," she said self-righteously. "No one would believe me."

"You told us he worked for S.K.U.N.K.," John Smith corrected her.

"Well, the CIA's as bad, if that's how it makes people behave."

"I'm inclined to agree with you, Aisling— unusual though that may be." He looked up at the cliff: Otis and Chris were already half-way up. "And that's why, as soon as they get out of sight, I intend to follow them. I'd like to make sure that, if our bomb-happy friend does manage to infiltrate (to pass through or into, as in filtering, Aisling—I did say you'd regret not bringing a good reference book with you)... Where was I? Oh yes: if Otis does manage to get into the radar station, I want to make sure he only lets in the right type of angels of mercy. Take the boat in to those rocks again, Erik. And then you and Aisling wait for the mist and try to get back to that village and raise the alarm. Not everybody in Iceland can be working for S.K.U.N.K. Just be careful."

Aisling stared at him. If he went too, there'd only be herself and Erik left, bobbing about in a small dinghy, with S.K.U.N.K. agents all over the place trying to catch them. She admitted to herself that she was scared stiff. "I thought you didn't fancy the idea of climbing that cliff," she objected.

"No more I do. But if that mutilator of the English language from the CIA can do it, we MI5-ers mustn't get left behind."

The sun was beginning to fade and the mist creep up as they watched John Smith jump onto the cliff ledge and start the climb upwards. But it wasn't just the fall in temperature that made Aisling shiver. She felt like one of the ten little Indian boys in the nursery rhyme: they'd started out with ten including Mulligan, and now there were only herself, Erik and Mulligan left. And Mulligan hardly counted. She looked back at the mist rolling in from the sea. Two little Indian boys, she whispered to herself, sitting in the sun; suddenly the mist came up, and then there was one.

Once again, Mulligan found himself being picked up and hugged tightly in Aisling's arms.

20
Reunion with Old Friends

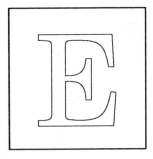

rik broke the silence first. "I suggest we explore the cave. Better to act than to mope, as my father would say. And we can't leave here until the fog comes up."

He started the engine and eased the boat slowly into the darkness. Wet rock shimmered in the reflected light from the waves and then both rock and water were inky black shadows. Erik cut the engine. "There may be rocks. Better to go safely with care than risk disaster with impetuosity. We shall push the boat along by hand for a bit and see how far we can get."

Aisling helped him move the boat forwards by pushing against the rock walls. They felt cold and clammy to her touch. She wondered if bats lived in sea caves. She shuddered.

"Shh!" Erik said urgently. "Do you hear anything?"

She listened. She heard the waves lapping against the side of the boat and whispering at the walls of the cave, the sound of the surf at the cave's mouth, the babble of the seabirds outside... And then she heard something else: a strange bumping sound. It seemed to come from the darkness ahead of them.

Images from horror films flashed through her mind: *King Kong, Gremlins, Jaws, The Monster from the Blue Lagoon...*

"Push forwards a bit more," Erik whispered.

The noises ahead became louder. Mulligan growled. *Irish cat fights off sea monster!* Aisling thought. It wasn't funny.

Erik nudged her and they held the boat still. Light was seeping like a halo round a black rock ahead. Carefully, they inched the boat nearer. Erik peered round the corner. He pulled his head back.

"Well?" whispered Aisling. "What is it?"

"Wait," Erik hissed, and started to push the boat back the way they had come. Once they were out of sight of the light, he stopped. His voice shook with excitement. "You'll never guess what's there!" he said.

"What?"

"The *Fafnir*! We've found the *Fafnir*!"

Aisling's heart leapt. "Is it all right? Did you see Seamus? Are your father and the others okay?"

"I could only see the ship. There's a quay there and the *Fafnir*'s moored alongside. The noise we heard is people loading crates onto a sort of train."

The wavelets continued to lap gently against the side of the cave. Mulligan snuggled his face into Aisling's stomach and curled up more comfortably.

"What do you think we should do?" she whispered.

"I think we should try to get aboard the ship and see what's happened, but I don't know if we can manage without being seen. The lights are very bright. I think... I think maybe I should try to swim to it."

"And leave me here?"

"You will have Mulligan. Anyway, someone must stay with the boat so that, if I get caught, you can go and get help at that village, like Mr Smith said. Give me, say, five minutes, and then get out as fast as you can."

"I don't know how to work the motor. It'd make more sense if I did the swimming." Aisling was surprised to hear herself volunteer.

There was nothing she wanted to do less than swim in that dark, murky water—quite apart from the danger of being caught by S.K.U.N.K. again. She hoped Erik would insist that he went.

"Perhaps you are right. Can you swim that far?"

Rats. He hadn't even argued. So much for chivalry, Aisling thought. "I've got medals for swimming," she said. "Look after Mulligan. I may, as Whatsisname Oates said to Captain Scott in the Antarctic, be gone some time."

They moved the boat forwards again, as far as they dared. Then Aisling kicked off her runners and let herself into the water. It was freezing! She turned away from the boat and swam towards the light, trying not to think of all the strange creatures which might be sharing the cold black water with her.

She stopped at the corner and trod water. Ahead of her, the cave broadened out into a sort of underground harbour and then narrowed again to form another tunnel at the end of which a light shone dimly. The *Fafnir*, her sail furled, her dragon prow gazing back towards Aisling, was moored at the quayside.

She took a deep breath and dived under water. The lights above her made a bright skin on the water surface. She headed for the dark shadow which was the ship. When her fingers touched wood, she surfaced, as slowly as possible, trying not to make any ripples. Gratefully, she filledher lungs with air again.

At the far side of the ship, the men continued working. No one had noticed her.

The rope Erik had let down for the fake policemen was still hanging from the stern. She grasped it and clambered up.

The deck of the *Fafnir* seemed horribly exposed and flooded with light. If anyone was on board, they must be in the cabin. She waited until she was sure no one was looking her way and then pulled herself up on deck, keeping Seamus's bed between herself and the quay. She wished it was the old brass bed from the studio: the mattress he was using here, even with his duvet on top of it, gave her very little cover. She lay down flat on the deck in the shadow of the bed and waited, her heart thudding, for the shout—or shots—which would show she'd been seen.

The men continued working.

She squirmed along the deck to the end of the bed. Then she got up into a crouch, steeling herself to dash across the deck to the shadow of the cabin.

A snort from above her made her freeze. She waited, her stomach in a tight knot, her muscles rigid, for Shavitov's huge paw to come down on her shoulder.

Instead there came a whisper from a voice she knew well. "Are you just passing through or do you have time to stop for a minute? I know my company may not be the most riveting, but I do sometimes have something worthwhile to say."

She turned, delighted. "Seamus!"

"Do you want to tell the whole of S.K.U.N.K. you're here? Mind you, I'm surprised, the way you were splashing about down there like a drunken porpoise, they haven't heard you already."

Aisling grinned. Seamus never changed. "Are you all right?" she asked. "Where are the others?"

"I am not all right. These uneducated, uncivilised, unspeakable imbeciles have trussed me up like a plucked chicken. At my age, it's disgraceful. I don't suppose you thought far enough ahead to bring a knife with you?"

Aisling had a vision of herself swimming through the dark water with a huge carving knife between her teeth and grinned. "Sorry," she said.

"Typical."

"Shall I see if I can untie you?"

"Better not for the moment. Until we see what we're going to do. Where are the rest of you?"

"Erik's waiting in a boat over there," Aisling pointed back the way she'd come. Fortunately, their cave was hardly visible in the gloom at the far side of the water. "And Otis, Chris and John Smith have gone to try to get back into a place S.K.U.N.K. have taken over on the cliffs."

"You've found their headquarters, then?"

"We don't know. We found something. Only I'm scared Otis is going to raise the magnetic barrier to let his nuclear bombers in before we can find the place they're making the earthquakes from. If he gets through, that is." She thought of the three men falling off the cliff, or walking straight into the arms of S.K.U.N.K. at the top, and shuddered. They were probably all prisoners—or dead—by now. "I liked Chris," she said, half to herself. "And Otis wasn't that bad, once you got to know him, and I suppose he's only carrying out orders."

It all seemed so hopeless. Even if she managed to release Seamus, he was still a cripple and would be more of a hindrance than a help to them. Either they'd all get caught again, or the others would succeed in letting the bombers through and they'd all be blown up anyway. Whatever happened, it didn't look good.

"Stop moping, child. We have to decide what to do next. Let me think for a moment."

"Where are Florence and Thorwald? And Archie? Are they okay?"

"How do you expect me to concentrate with you rabbiting on all the time?"

Aisling controlled her impatience. She waited, shivering, for what seemed like hours. "Erik's only going to wait five minutes, and then he's going to try and get help," she pointed out.

"Hmm. Well, I suppose it's the best we can do, probably. I doubt very much if Florence could make it that far and I know neither Thorwald nor Archie can swim. Typical of seamen that: not to learn the one thing that could save your life. However. What you'll have to do is—*To be or not to be? That is the question.*" Seamus raised his voice. "*Whether 'tis nobler in the mind...*"

Aisling thought he'd gone mad. Then she heard steps on deck and threw herself flat alongside the mattress. Seamus rolled over so that part of the duvet slipped towards her. *"...to suffer the slings and arrows of outrageous fortune..."*

She pulled it over her back as best she could and lay motionless, her skin crawling, her mouth dry with fear.

"You are up to zomezink, Grandaddy, no? You tells Shavitov vat you are doing, yes?"

"Or to take arms against a sea of troubles... I thought even an intellectual nincompoop like yourself would recognize *Hamlet*, but I obviously assumed too much." Seamus sighed sarcastically.

There was the sound of a blow. "You stop taking ze Mockey, yes? I do not understand vy the boss is not keeling you, but ve are very nearly feeneeshed now. Ve make one more earthquake. California, she falls into ze sea, no? And Europe, she blows apart. Zen zey gives us vat ve vants. And zen..."

Aisling tried not to shiver at the menace in his tone.

"Oh go jump in a volcano," Seamus muttered wearily.

"I go. But I do not forget."

Heavy footsteps pounded across the deck again and disappeared.

Aisling raised her head. "Are you all right?" she whispered.

"Fine," said Seamus. To her horror, she saw blood trickling out of a gash at the corner of his mouth. Seamus tried to smile and grimaced with pain. "Now, as I was saying: how far is it to this boat of yours?"

"Not far. Just over there."

"Good. They've almost finished loading those crates. You go back to Erik. Do you think you can swim with that rope there?" He pointed to a coil of rope beside the tiller.

"I think so."

"Hmm. You'll have to. Tie one end to something—that stuck up dragon at the front will do—and take the other end back to Erik. When they've finished here and it's quiet again, pull your boat alongside. That way you won't make any noise. If you can tie the boat to something at the other end, so much the better—it'll help you get back without raising the alarm. Thorwald, Hansie, Archie and Florence are all prisoners in the cabin there. Cut them loose and take them back with you. As soon as you're clear, start the engine and go for help."

"What about you?"

"Too much bother. Just leave me here—I'll

be fine. Don't argue, girl—as you pointed out yourself, Erik won't wait much longer. Now, tie that rope round you and go."

Swimming back with the heavy rope was not easy—the distance seemed twice as far as before. The rope dragged at her and threatened to pull her under: *Young Irish swimmer drowned in Icelandic cave...*

But finally Erik's pale anxious face peered out of the gloom ahead of her. He helped her into the boat. The first part of the plan had worked and no one had noticed her. Would the second part be as easy?

Hours seemed to pass before the men left the quay. Two remained on guard, each armed with a machine gun. Aisling was relieved when one of them brought out a deck of cards and they sat down on a couple of crates which hadn't yet been loaded into the wagons and started to play.

"Now!" she whispered.

They pulled themselves across the water by the rope. Even though they made no noise, they were horribly visible in the glow of the overhead lights. If the men looked up...

They reached the shelter of the *Fafnir* and climbed on board. The guards were still playing cards.

Holding their breath, they slipped across thedeck to the cabin. Seamus could wait till last.

It was dark inside. Surely, if a S.K.U.N.K. guard was there, he'd hardly be sitting in the dark? "Is there anybody there?" Aisling whispered.

"Aisling! Well, isn't that a nice surprise! Thank goodness you're all right—I was worrying quite badly about you. I hope you've been looking after yourself properly and getting enough to eat. And is that Erik you have with you? There you are, Thorwald, Erik is safe too. Isn't that nice?"

"Do not give up hope until you have seen the corpse. I knew they would turn up. Find a knife and cut these ropes, and then we can see what we can do."

"That's an afa' lot better. It's guid to see you, Erik lad. And you, too, Aisling." Archie rubbed his ankles and stood up. He helped Florence to her feet. "Are ye okay, lass? The divils didna' hurt ye, did they? If they did,they'll hae me, Archie McTavish, to answer to."

"Thanks, Archie. I'm fine. Have you freed Hansie too, Aisling?"

Aisling hadn't noticed Hansie in the cabin. She quickly cut him free also. "Thank you.

That is, as Archie said, a lot better. You must be Aisling, Seamus's godchild. And this must be Erik. You are blessed, Thorwald, to have so fine a son."

"A man's wealth is in his cattle and his children, as the old saying goes. I am indeed lucky." Thorwald put his arm proudly round Erik's shoulders.

"Will I cut Seamus free too? He told me not to before, so as not to raise suspicions. In fact..." she paused, "he said to leave him and just rescue you. We can't do that, can we?"

"Naturally not. We must..."

"Shh!" interrupted Erik urgently. "Someone's coming."

A black shape appeared at the top of the cabin steps. With a delighted "prrrriau" it jumped down towards them, flung itself at Florence, licked her nose and then jumped off to sit expectantly in front of the galley. Mulligan was hungry again.

Aisling picked him up. "He must have got tired of waiting. I didn't think he could climb a rope, though."

"Yon cat is capable o' onything," Archie said dourly.

"Have you any idea where we are?" Thorwald asked. "We have been kept prisoner here since the ship was captured."

Erik described the underwater tunnel which led from the sea, past the quay where they were moored and along to the brightly-lit area further inside the cliff. "We can't see what's up there, but I think that's where all the people are. We had better stay well away from it. We'll have to go back the way we came. Unfortunately, there was nothing in the tunnel to tie the rope onto, so I'll have to start the engine again to get out."

"Hmm. When there is no alternative, one must choose the one way left. A man's life is no longer than his allotted span, and we may perhaps get away before they realize what is happening. What do you think, Hansie? You know this region. Have you any idea where this tunnel could be?"

"There are many caves under the cliffs of Snaefellsness. But I have never had occasion to enter any of them. I agree with you, however, my friend: we will have to start the engine and risk alerting S.K.U.N.K. But first I should like to see this 'brightly-lit area' Erik mentioned. We have been looking for this gang's base every since we discovered what they were up to, and we have found nothing yet. Here, they could remain hidden for a long time."

"We've found their base already," Erik said eagerly. "John Smith and Otis are there now with Chris."

"We hope," Aisling corrected, her fingers crossed.

"It's a radar station on top of the cliff further north. Otis thinks that's where they work the magnetic shield from and it could be the headquarters of their whole operation."

"Otis is still muttering about letting in his precious air force to bomb the place flat," Aisling said bitterly. "John Smith was going to try to stop him and bring in conventional forces instead. I hope he gets there first."

There was silence for a minute. Then Hansie spoke again. Aisling couldn't help noticing how he, Thorwald and even Erik spoke excellent English. She thought of her fluency in French and was glad no one could see her blushing in the dark. She really must work harder at languages when they got home—*if* they got home she thought.

Hansie was still speaking. "We did check that radar station out some time ago but, although there had been a change of staff, it was convincingly explained and we saw nothing suspicious. Maybe my men will have checked it again: I imagine they have stepped up their operations since this morning."

"Hansie and his family were captured just after I phoned," Thorwald explained. "S.K.U.N.K. must have been tapping his phone lines."

"I told everyone Olga was a spy, even before we found her transmitting that message, but nobody would believe me."

"True, Aisling." She could tell Thorwald was smiling. "The voice of the owl is sometimes mistaken for the foolish chattering of a magpie. But once she had seen the *Fafnir*, she would have guessed anyway what we intended."

"Seamus said the same," Aisling admitted. "Which reminds me—Seamus! We've forgotten all about him. He's still lying tied up on deck."

"You are right. We will untie him and move him to your little boat. It has an outboard motor, I imagine? We will be able to escape more quickly in that than in the *Fafnir*."

"How many guards are there?" Hansie asked.

"Two. They were playing cards when we came alongside."

"Have we got any weapons?"

"They took them all, I think." Florence's gentle voice sounded disappointed. "Even my crossbow—though I doubt if any of them knows how to use it."

Archie chuckled. "I'll bet they dinna, lassie."

"There are knives in the cutlery drawer," Aisling suggested. "I used one of them to cut you free."

"Good. Now. We have to take care of these guards first, before we do anything else. Archie, you stay and look after the others. Thorwald, come with me."

Aisling couldn't resist peering carefully round the cabin door. The guards were still playing cards. Thorwald and Hansie slipped onto the quay and crouched behind a couple of crates. Hansie picked up something and threw it towards the guards. It landed beyond them, making them turn round in alarm. They reached for their machine guns.

And then Thorwald and Hansie were on top of them. For two elderly men, they moved surprisingly fast, Aisling thought.

They stood back. The guards fell like broken puppets at their feet. If she ever got home again, Aisling decided, she would certainly take up karate.

Florence was bathing Seamus's face while Aisling rubbed his wrists and ankles as Thorwald came back to the *Fafnir*. Hansie had stayed on the quay to examine the crates which had been loaded onto the wagons waiting on the track.

"Are they dead?" Aisling asked as he came on board.

"Every man must die one day. Now, let's move Seamus onto your boat."

"First you'll have a nice cup of tea and a bite to eat," Florence said firmly. "I've put thekettle on."

"When we are finished here. Danger is best confronted on an empty stomach."

"Rubbish."

Thorwald smiled. "You make the tea, Florence, while we transfer what we need to the dinghy." He winked at Aisling. "Even the mightiest oak knows when to bend with the wind."

Footsteps sounded on the quay at the far side of the cabin. Aisling froze. Could someone else from S.K.U.N.K. have come back?

But it was only Hansie. "These wagons are filled with explosives," he said. "I am curious as to why they are here. And what is at the end of the tunnel. I think I shall go and find out."

"I'll come wi' ye," Archie volunteered. "I could do wi' stretching my legs."

Thorwald looked at the others worriedly. "I think we should get them out of here to safety first. One should not ask more of a pony than it is willing to carry."

"Hmph." Seamus snorted. "Just who are you calling a pony? If you're worried about Florence and myself and those two children there, don't be. You go off and enjoy yourselves playing detectives. We'll start a game of Trivial Pursuits or I-Spy or something equally demanding, just to prove to ourselves we are intelligent human beings rather than millstones round your necks."

Thorwald grinned. "Did I ever doubt your intelligence, old friend? But I think, all the same, I shall leave Archie with you. He is very good at Trivial Pursuits I think, are you not, Archie?"

Och aye," Archie said sarcastically. He looked gently at Florence. "I dinna mind staying," he said. "If you're no back, I'll tak' them tae safety, dinna fear. And I'll enjoy a cup o' tea and a bite to eat while we're waiting for you."

Florence smiled back. "It's a pleasure to cook for you, Archibald."

Aisling looked at Erik and raised her eyebrows. He grinned back.

21
Mulligan Catches a Rat

lorence had been right and Thorwald wrong, Aisling thought as she finished a meal of bacon and scrambled eggs: she did feel a lot better with some warm food inside her. Mulligan agreed too. He curled up on Seamus's bed, his bloated stomach sticking out like a fur-covered orange balloon, and purred happily.

He was disgusted when Archie pushed him off so that they could move Seamus and his mattress into the dinghy. He spat and leapt over the side of the *Fafnir* to land on the quay.

Erik stared worriedly at the entrance to the tunnel. "My father and Hansie should be back by now. What is keeping them?"

"I dinna ken, laddie. But we'll gie them a few minutes yet."

Once Seamus was safely installed in the dinghy, along with the essential stores which Florence, despite Archie's complaints, refused to leave behind, Aisling looked for Mulligan.

"He's probably back on the *Fafnir*, hoping we've left something there he can eat," Florence suggested. "You'd better go and get him before the others come back."

Aisling searched the *Fafnir*: there was no sign of him. She jumped ashore and peered along the tunnel towards the light in the distance. What on earth were Thorwald and Hansie doing? They should have been back ages ago.

"Mulligan," she called softly. "Puss, puss! Come on, Mulligan!"

A scream from behind the train of wagons made the hair prickle on the back of her neck—she understood what people meant when they talked about someone's blood running cold. She almost had a heart attack when Erik suddenly appeared beside her, and had to grab hold of the nearest wagon to steady herself. "Don't ever creep up on me like that again!" she hissed.

"Did you hear a noise?" he whispered.

The blood-curdling shriek was repeated. Then silence returned like a shroud.

Aisling looked at the bodies of the two guards on the quay. They were lying just where they'd fallen. Surely they couldn't have made that awful noise? "It sounded like...I don't know...like someone being tortured."

"You're to come back," Erik said shakily. "Archie thinks we've waited long enough and wants to go now."

"But what about Mulligan? And your father and Hansie?" Aisling wondered fearfully if the ghastly scream had had anything to do with them, and just stopped herself in time from saying so to Erik. She hoped he didn't think it himself.

"We will have to leave them." Erik kept his voice steady. "If they have been caught, we must get help."

"They'll be waiting for us outside the cave— the people from the radar station and the helicopter...They've probably caught John Smith and Chris and Otis too. We'll never get out of here!"

"We won't if you don't hurry up. Come on!"

"I've got to get Mulligan." Aisling looked desperately down the quay.

Something moved behind one of the crates. Then a small dark object scurried out into the open. An orange shape followed it, pounced and then batted it back into the shadows. "It's Mulligan! He's caught a rat! That must be what was screaming. I won't be a minute."

She pulled herself free and ran down the quay, stumbling on the rail tracks set into the concrete. Mulligan snatched the rat up in his mouth and retreated, growling possessively, behind the wagons. It screamed again.

"Come on, Mulligan. You can't be hungry, you've only just eaten. Leave it and come out. Or we'll have to leave without you."

She looked back at Erik. He signalled to Archie in the boat and ran up to join her. "Go round the back," she whispered. "Try to push him out. I'll catch him this side."

Suddenly there was a rumbling from the tunnel. She stood up to see what it was—and then quickly sank down again to cower in the gap between the wagons, her heart beating like a set of drums against her ribs. A low truck had trundled out of the tunnel mouth. There were at least three people in it and one of them was built like a gorilla: Shavitov had come back.

He seemed to be swearing in his own language. Even though he kept his voice to a whisper, shivers ran down Aisling's spine. "So zat ees how zey escaped," he said to whoever was with him. "Ve vill make zem pay for eet, yes?"

They must have discovered the guards' bodies.

Terrified, Aisling shrank back still further into the shadow between the wagons.

"You looks in ze sheep, yes?" Shavitov ordered. "I keeps you covered."

She saw a couple of men, with machine guns at the ready, board the *Fafnir*. Had Erik seen them? Would he do something? She knew she ought to shout out and warn Archie—he might still have time to start the engine and get away—but the sound of Shavitov's heavy breathing, just a couple of feet away, paralysed her completely. *Aisling Daly saves the world!* Some hope, she thought bitterly. She despised herself for being such a coward. She couldn't just watch the others be taken prisoner again and do nothing... And yet here she was standing shaking, her mouth so dry she couldn't even croak a warning, while the two men, having found the *Fafnir* deserted, jumped down into the dinghy.

The silence was shattered as the engine roared into life. Aisling's hopes soared: maybe Archie had managed to get them away in time after all!

And then the dinghy, with one of the S.K.U.N.K. men at the tiller and the other covering Florence and Archie with a machine gun, came round beneath the dragon figurehead of the *Fafnir* and stopped alongside the quay.

"The other three are here!" the man shouted. "What will we do with them?"

"Ve vill take zem to ze control room, no? Zey hav been of no uses to us—ve should hav keeled zem long ago. But ve shall do so now—very slowly. Yes?"

Shavitov climbed aboard the dinghy which rocked violently as his huge weight hit it. The man at the tiller opened the throttle and the boat disappeared into the tunnel at the end of the quay, a diminishing black shape against the distant light.

Aisling waited a minute and then stood up. She was trembling. Erik came round the wagons towards her.

"We should have left," he said bitterly. "I knew I shouldn't have let you waste time looking for Mulligan. We'd have been safely out of here by now, getting help, if you hadn't messed things up."

"Why didn't you do anything then," she asked peevishly. She knew she was only getting at him because she felt guilty herself. "You just watched them take Seamus and Florence and Archie away. You're not so fantastic either, are you?"

Erik sighed. "Let us not argue. When the wolf has stolen the chicken it is pointless to worry about who shut the coop. We have to decide what to do now. Father and Hansie must be in trouble, or they would have come back. And goodness knows what has happened to Mr Smith and the others. So that just leaves us. We have to get help somehow."

"We could take the *Fafnir*," Aisling suggested.

"By ourselves? Perhaps, once we got her out to sea, we might just manage to handle her. As long as it wasn't too windy. But how do we get her out to sea?"

"Couldn't we row?"

"Two of us would never manage it."

They were silent for a moment, each thinking their own thoughts. Mulligan, deciding all of a sudden that the rat had become boring, came to rub up against Aisling's leg. She picked him up and put him on her shoulder. It always made her feel better to have Mulligan to hold—like the blanket Linus sucks in the *Peanuts* cartoon, she thought wryly: *Intrepid Irish heroine my left foot!*

"What will we do, then?" she asked.

Erik straightened his shoulders. "We can only do what we are able to—but we may be able to do more than we think: one of Dad's favourite sayings. We will have to go up that tunnel and see what the situation is. We may be able to help the others. We can only try."

Aisling held Mulligan tightly as she followed Erik along the narrow railway track which filled the ledge between the tunnel wall and the sea. She assumed that the rails were for transporting stuff from the quay to wherever the tunnel led to. She only hoped they wouldn't send another truck down to bring up the wagons waiting there: the only way to avoid being run down would be to jump into the dark water below.

They reached the end of the tunnel. There was a truck there, waiting to go down to the quay, and they hid behind it. Carefully, they raised their heads and looked.

22
Inside the Volcano

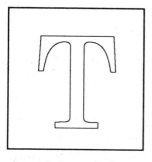

hey were in a huge underground cave—much bigger than the one they'd just left. It reminded Aisling of the headquarters S.K.U.N.K. had built in Switzerland. It, too, had been inside a mountain—but this time they were in the crater of a volcano and sheer walls rose to a circular glass roof, tinted brown, no doubt to look like earth to any plane flying over it. Apart from a small harbour at the entrance to the tunnel, the bottom of the crater was floored and formed a vast power house, full of instruments and panels of winking lights. Aisling felt as if she was caught in a nightmare: the whole place looked as if a giant had raided a very advanced space station and plonked it down in the middle of a volcano like a set of Lego for him to play with. The machines and banks of instruments, the technicians in their white coats, the armed guards patrolling the perimeter—all were dwarfed by the immensity of the natural phenomenon. If this was S.K.U.N.K.'s headquarters, it was no wonder Hansie's police had never found it.

The dinghy was moored at the entrance to the tunnel, alongside the police launch. Aisling wondered why the *Fafnir* hadn't been brought this far too, but then realised that the tunnel was too low and narrow for anything but a very small boat to get through. An additional safety factor, she thought with grudging admiration.

She looked for the others, but couldn't see them. Seamus's mattress was still in the dinghy, but he himself had been removed. What had S.K.U.N.K. done with them all? She remembered Shavitov's threats—were they too late already?

Suddenly a voice, sounding as if it were only a foot or two away, made them both squeeze back to where the shadows were deepest. It was Lerntowski: he must be just round the corner, out of sight.

"I should have killed you when you first interfered with my plans," he squeaked in his expressionless high-pitched voice. "But I am a man who dislikes violence."

"If that is so," Florence interrupted (she sounded at her most school-teacherish)... "if that is so, then why did you allow that oversized unmannerly lout there to treat my brother like that? He needs medical help. I suggest you find a doctor for him. Immediately."

Lerntowski ignored her. "You people are like gnats. You annoy me with your little pinprick bites. Up till now, I have just brushed you away, but perhaps I should have taken my colleague Shavitov's advice..." the voice hissed like a snake poised to strike, "and exterminated you completely, as one exterminates a gnat when it is too bothersome." There was a noise of two hands slapping violently together. "So."

Aisling shivered.

"I keel zem now, no?" Shavitov asked eagerly.

"Why not? We..."

There was a commotion at the other side of the crater.

"Go and find out what is happening," Lerntowski ordered.

At first they could see nothing, then Shavitov's huge bulk came into view opposite them. He was waddling towards a dark shadow in the crater wall—which must have been another tunnel, Aisling thought, as a group of guards suddenly materialized, as if from nowhere, in front of it. A slim figure stepped out from between them—it was Olga! She said something to Shavitov as she passed him. His head went up like a pointer's and he stared towards the tunnel. Then he turned and waddled back behind Olga and they both disappeared from sight again behind the curve in the crater wall.

"Well?" they heard Lerntowski ask as Olga and Shavitov reached him.

"Ze police are at ze radar station!" Olga reported. "Zey hav broken through ze fence and are at ze main building. I hav ordered ze men to fight, but zey are outnumbered. Soon zey vill be in and zen—pouf! Ze barrier vill be removed. Ze planes vill come in and..."

"Control yourself. No one can harm us here. We can defend both entrances until our work is done."

"But you do not know! Zey vere talking of ze nuclear bomb! Viz a nuclear bomb zey could shatter ze whole mountain!"

"I see." Lerntowski spoke as unemotionally as ever. "Go and tell Petrocelli to get ready to start the next shock. This time we will split the

Atlantic in half as we promised. I shall send a last message to Moscow and Washington. They will give in, never fear."

"Vat about zees peoples?" Shavitov asked.

"You may stay here and guard them." Lerntowski sounded as if he might be smiling. "I am sure you will not allow them to trouble us again."

Olga came into their field of vision and crossed the cavern to speak to one of the men in white coats. Lerntowski appeared after her and went to what seemed to be a special kind of radio transmitter near the other entrance. Erik touched Aisling's arm and pulled her back into the tunnel.

"We've got to do something!" he whispered.

"What?"

"I don't know. The launch is just over there. If you can distract them, I may be able to get to it and go for help. The police are at the radar station, Olga said—I could go there."

"Let's try something else first," Aisling heard herself saying. "There's only Shavitov here at the moment."

She took Mulligan from her shoulder and pushed him out of the tunnel. "Go on, Mulligan," she whispered. "Find Florence. Florence has food. She'll feed you."

Mulligan gave her an inquiring look over his shoulder, put his tail up like a banner and walked delicately out into the light.

"So," Shavitov was saying. "I must zeenk, yes? Vich von of you vill I keel first? Perhaps ze woman, no? Vill I sleet her throat? Or... GO AVAY, HORRIBLE ZING!" And then, to Aisling's delight, he suddenly started to sneeze.

"Now!" Aisling whispered.

"They crept round the corner of the truck. Shavitov, purple in the face, was bent over double, gasping for air. Mulligan walked away from him and rubbed up against Florence who was tied, with Thorwald, Hansie and Archie, to a metal bar let into the rock wall. Seamus was propped up against the wall beside them, his face pale and bruised, his hands strapped behind his back, grinning with pleasure as he watched Shavitov suffer.

"And about time, too," he snorted as Erik cut him loose. "I was wondering what was keeping you two. Now, will somebody deal with that oversized disgrace to humanity so that we can get out of here before everybody goes mad."

Hansie stepped forwards and hit Shavitov sharply across the back of the neck, just as he and Thorwald had dealt with the guards at the quay. Shavitov stopped sneezing and slumped to the ground.

There was a moment's complete silence. It had all happened so quickly that the people in the crater had been taken by surprise. Now they started to react. Someone shouted. People started moving towards them.

Aisling saw Thorwald hoist Seamus over his shoulder, Archie picked up Florence (who didn't complain, she noticed in surprise) and then Erik pushed her into the launch after them. While Hansie and Thorwald shouted something to each other in Norwegian, Archie untied the dinghy's painter and fastened it to the launch so that no one could use it to follow them. Thorwald started the motor and they roared off into the tunnel. Shots exploded behind them and ricocheted off the tunnel roof. Erik, who had picked up Shavitov's machine gun, fired back.

"We've forgotten Hansie!" Aisling shouted above the roar of the engine.

Thorwald said nothing, but his face was grim.

They stopped at the quay beside the *Fafnir*. On Thorwald's orders, Archie untied the dinghy and fastened it to the stern of the *Fafnir*. Then he attached the *Fafnir* to the back of the launch.

Thorwald caught Aisling's eye. "It is a bad captain who deserts his ship," he explained.

"We don't have time for all that!" Aisling appealed to Florence. "If we don't get out fast, they'll catch up with us." She heard a rumble in the tunnel. "That's them coming after us now! Why don't we go?"

"We're waiting for Hansie," Archie explained. "That'll be him noo."

A truck raced out of the tunnel and screamed to a halt in a shower of sparks. Hansie jumped out. He pulled a lever and the truck backed into the tunnel again, gaining speed as it disappeared. There was a confused noise of shouting, some shots... Somebody screamed in the tunnel.

Hansie jumped into the launch and, with the *Fafnir* bobbing along in their wake like a ridiculous dragon-headed wooden duck, they roared away from the quay towards the cave Aisling and Erik had come in by, it seemed years ago.

It was marvellous to reach the open sea and feel the breeze and see the sky again. Aisling looked back. The cliff reared up behind them and, beyond, the snow-capped summit of Snaefellsjökul glowed a rosy pink as the sun set at the edge of the northern horizon. Olga had said that the police had stormed the radar station: did that mean that John Smith and the others had managed to climb the cliff and were alive?

"Are we going to the radar station now?" she asked.

Her words were drowned out by a huge explosion behind them. She turned. The noise seemed to come both from the cave they'd just left and from the top of the mountain. Black smoke rose from the volcano. Another explosion sounded—and another.

Thorwald clapped Hansie on the shoulder. "Well done, my friend."

"I don't think their equipment will have survived that," Hansie answered with satisfaction. "Let us hope they didn't have time to set off their last earthquake."

"How did you do that?" Aisling asked, awestruck.

"Thorwald and I discovered that the wagons were filled with eplosives. It was just a matter of laying a fuse."

Erik grinned. "I doubt if even Otis's bombers would have been as effective."

Otis's bombers! Aisling suddenly remembered what Olga had said in the crater. She grabbed Thorwald's arm. "We have to stop them! Olga said they're on their way!"

"We have, child. Do you not understand? S.K.U.N.K. can do no more harm—for the moment, anyway. It is too much to hope that a leopard will change his spots: although one may have drawn the fangs of the serpent, it would be a rash man who would think that he had tamed it."

Aisling groaned in exasperation. "Not S.K.U.N.K.," she said. "The bombers! They're coming with nuclear bombs to flatten the whole of Snaefellsness or whatever it's called."

"They'll see the smoke," Erik said hopefully.

"I'm nae so sure, laddie." Archie shook his head.

"No one would be so criminal," Hansie observed. "Not even S.K.U.N.K. Do they not know the damage it will cause—to man, to nature, to the land itself? For hundreds of years?"

"They don't care," Aisling muttered. "People like Otis and that American captain I met. They go on about 'limited strategic use and target accuracy' and all sorts of phrases that make them feel better, and then they think that everything will be all right."

Hansie looked south worriedly. Clouds were gathering on the horizon, black ominous shadows against a sky still streaked with blue and pink and purple. "We must tell them what we have done. We will go to the radar station. Let us hope S.K.U.N.K. have not destroyed the radio transmitters there."

They raced across the blood-streaked water to the radar station. They passed the small cove with the hut again and Aisling wondered if Shavitov had already escaped (or been released) when they had passed it before—was it only that afternoon? It seemed like centuries ago. "If we leave the *Fafnir* here, we'll be able to go a muckle bit quicker," Archie suggested. Thorwald agreed, and they put in hastily to the pier, tied the *Fafnir* fast, and continued north again.

They landed at the same beach they had used before. Florence decided to stay in the launch to look after Seamus whom she had been nursing in the cabin. The others climbed the steep hill to the road. The skuas were even more vicious than Aisling had remembered, but she paid little attention to them: her mind was on the radar station and what they would find there.

23
Bombers

man in the uniform of
the Icelandic police was
at the barrier. Aisling
thought for one terrible moment that it was
another S.K.U.N.K. agent in disguise; she was
relieved when he saluted Hansie and raised
the barrier to let them through.

Hansie spoke to him urgently. He replied,
gesturing towards the radar station ahead of
them.

Erik grabbed Hansie's arm. "Listen!" he
said.

At first Aisling could hear nothing but the
pounding of the surf on the rocks below and
the scream of the seabirds. Then she heard it:
a low droning sound coming from the south.

"Come on!" Thorwald raced across the short
grass to the main building. It was surrounded

by Icelandic soldiers. The glass of the entrance hall was shattered, the doors had been kicked down. A body lay motionless, in a corner. Aisling forced herself to look at it: thank goodness it wasn't Chris or John Smith.

As she followed the others to the main control room, someone shouted her name. She turned. Chris was running down the corridor towards them. He picked her up and spun her round. "It's great to see you and Erik again, Aisling. We were hoping you were okay. So you've found Hansie and Thorwald. And Archie. Fit like, my auld freen'?"

"Richt fine, laddie," Archie replied with a grin. "An it's guid tae see you again, too."

Chris looked round. "What about Florence and Seamus? Are they all right?"

"They're safe, too, Chris. But where's Otis? We have to stop him. We've destroyed S.K.U.N.K.'s headquarters—we've come to get him to turn back the bombers."

"Thank God for that. John's been arguing with him inside there. I left them at it and came to see if I could find Olga. You haven't seen her anywhere have you? I've searched this whole building."

Aisling looked away.

"We will speak to you later, Christopher,"

Thorwald said quietly. "Now we must find Otis."

He led the way along the corridor.

As they got to the door of the main control room, Hansie stopped abruptly. Aisling peered round his shoulder.

Otis was standing at the main console with a radio receiver in one hand. In the other he held his knife. It was touching the side of John Smith's neck.

"Aha." John Smith had been lolling back, seemingly totally at ease, in a swivel chair. He looked up as they came in. "Mafeking has been relieved. Check your history of the Boer War, Aisling, for the reference. It's good to see you, gentlemen. And lady. Perhaps you will be able to make our bomb-happy American cousin here see reason—I have been arguing with him until my face is as blue as a baboon's bottom, to no avail. Strange as it may seem to the rest of you, my powers of persuasion seem to be waning."

Thorwald stepped past Hansie into the room. Otis tightened his grip on the knife. "This is a crisis situation, bud. I am going to be up front with you: I intend to let these bombers do their duty. The world must be made safe for democracy, at any price, ecology-wise."

"If that's the price of your democracy, I think I'd prefer to do without it," John Smith said conversationally.

"There is no longer any need, my friend," Hansie interrupted. "S.K.U.N.K. can do no more harm. We have blown up their equipment. I suggest you call your bombers off before it is too late. It would be very embarrassing for your President if he wiped out a friendly nation for no reason, would it not?"

"Uhuh." Otis looked thoughtful. "You're talking a whole new ballgame, here. If you're right, that is."

"He *is* right." Aisling said. "Just look out of the window at the volcano there. Do you see the smoke coming out of it? That's where they had their headquarters—nobody could be alive in there any more."

John Smith looked out of the window too. In the distance, Snaefellsjökul was belching out clouds of smoke and ashes. He whistled. "That volcano is alive and indubitably kicking! How in the name of the little green man did you manage to reactivate a volcano, Thorwald my old friend?"

"Hansie's eplosive must have found a weak spot in the crater floor. A man may act, but the result of his action is in the lap of the gods.

S.K.U.N.K. will certainly trouble us no more."

Otis stared at the volcano in amazement. "All right," he said slowly. "You have me persuaded, S.K.U.N.K.-wise. Hold on a minute while I access Bomber Command."

He spoke into the microphone: "OW to Daisy Duck. OW to Daisy Duck. Do you read me?"

The speaker on the console in front of him crackled. "Daisy Duck here. Hearing you loud and clear. Can see the target right ahead."

"Abort mission!" ordered Otis. "I repeat: abort mission!"

Aisling breathed a sigh of relief. They had got there in time.

"You sure?" the voice on the radio asked. It sounded disappointed.

"Affirmative. Divert to Reykjavik and land there. I shall meet with you presently. Over and out."

The pilot sighed. "All right, bud. If you say so. A pity, though—I was rather looking forwards to using one of these things at last. Still...over and out."

Otis put down the microphone and stood up. "There we are, then, folks. Mission accomplished, as they say. I look forwards to sharing with you your experiences in the context of your upper-handing S.K.U.N.K., strategically-wise. At this moment in time, however, I must take a rain check. I have to go to Reykjavik to meet with my boys."

"We will come with you," said Hansie. "It is time these good people had a taste of Icelandic hospitality. They have not had much of an occasion to enjoy our beautiful island so far: it is the least we can do to thank them."

"One does not judge a barrel of apples by the rotten ones," Thorwald said. "But a warm bath and a good meal would not go amiss."

Aisling couldn't have agreed with him more.

24
Journey to Valhalla

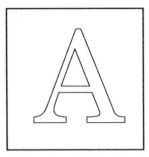s they were leaving the
control room they heard
raised voices from
further along the corridor. There was a sound
of scuffling. And then footsteps came steadily
towards them. Three people turned the corner.

Aisling's blood froze: it was Shavitov and
Lerntowski, with Olga behind them.

Then she realized they had their hands up.
She relaxed. They must have tried to escape
through the passage joining the crater to the
radar station, which Olga had used earlier.
And they'd walked straight into the arms of
the Icelandic police.

"Take them to Reykjavik," Hansie ordered.
"They will stand trial there."

Shavitov glared at them. Aisling looked
away quickly. She had never seen such naked

hatred: it made her feel like a mouse trapped by a stoat. She hoped sincerely that he wouldn't get out of prison again this time—his vengeance would be terrible. She was glad when a policeman moved them on.

"Olga!" Chris appeared from the other end of the corridor. "Thank goodness I've found you! I was looking for you everywhere!" Then he noticed the policemen and Shavitov and Lerntowski. "What's going on?" His voice came out as a urgent squeak.

Olga turned to smile at him, her dark slanting eyes bright, her perfect teeth showing in a smile. "Goodbye, Christopher," she murmured huskily. "Eet ees a pity ve could not both hav been on ze same side, no?"

"You really do work for S.K.U.N.K.?"

"Of course. You vant I should be ze meek leetle housevife? Me, Olga Shostavuishina! You are a fool, my Christopher. A sweet fool, but a fool all ze same. Adieu." One of the policemen nudged her with his pistol. She threw him a look of contempt, blew Chris a kiss and walked haughtily away.

Chris ran his fingers through his long curly hair. He looked so hurt that Aisling was tempted to cuddle him like a little child. She grinned: she doubted if he'd appreciate it—he preferred his women mature.

"Well, that is over. No man knows the outcome of an action or when a day will be his last; but we have been successful this time, my friends, and we—and the rest of the world— can go to bed tonight in peace. I must get back to my ship. Archie, Erik—are you ready to leave? And perhaps Chris will give us a hand until we pick up more crew in Reykjavik."

"You'd better come with me, Ash," John Smith suggested. "I'm sure Hansie can spare one of his men to drive us to Reykjavik—it'll be quicker than the boat. We'll put you on the first plane out—your mother must be worrying herself sick about you by now."

With a guilty start, Aisling remembered that her parents still thought she was staying with Catherine at Carlingford. John Smith was right: the sooner she got home, the better. Though she'd miss Erik and the others. She grinned. She remembered how she'd disliked Erik when she'd first met him. "Will you be coming to Ireland again, Thorwald?" she asked.

"We do not know what the future has in store for us. But, if the gods are willing, we will indeed come and, as our American friend here would say, visit with you, hospitality-wise."

Otis laughed. "You're a great guy, Thorwald.

I've enjoyed working with you. And if you're ever in the States with that archaic dragon-headed bathtub of yours, do come and visit with me. I look forwards to having an eyeball-to-eyeball interface situation with you again. At any moment in time."

Otis hadn't turned out so bad after all, Aisling thought. It was strange to think that, after today, she'd never see him again. She remembered how suspicious she'd been of him in Dalkey. Which reminded her: "Why were you spying on Seamus in Dalkey, Otis?" she asked. "It doesn't make sense if you belong to the CIA."

John Smith raised an eyebrow. "Spying on Seamus? Tell me more!"

"You smuggled a microphone into his studio somehow and were eavesdropping on his conversations. I know because I saw you hiding in the house next door."

"Congratulations, Aisling. You'd make a good agent yourself, securitywise. As I told you on that charming trip we undertook together to...what was the name of that cute little port? Carlingford?...we thought, in the context of maximising our alternatives, that Seamus might come up with a way to beat S.K.U.N.K. He refused to have a meaningful dialogue with us, so we had to resort to covert means, listeningwise. I sure am sorry that it led to a less than open interface between us." He put out his hand. "I trust we're buddies now?"

"There's something I wanted to ask," Erik intervened. "How did you escape from the *Fafnir* this morning when the rest of us were caught?"

"Easy, bud. I just kept a low profile while our friends were accessising the ship and slipped overboard. It wasn't that far, distancewise, to swim to the shore."

John Smith grinned at them. "Come on, you two. Let's get out of here. We can discuss all this in Reykjavik. *After* we've had a hot bath and a good meal."

As they came out of the building, Lerntowski, Shavitov and Olga were being put aboard a police landrover.

Suddenly, Shavitov whirled round and smashed the gun out of the hand of the policeman behind him. Olga raised her arm; something bright glinted in her hand; and the driver of the landrover slumped across the wheel. She pushed him aside. Lerntowski helped Shavitov aboard, and the landrover roared through the broken perimeter fence. Soldiers and policemen fired after them, but the landrover drove on. Hansie jumped into an armoured car with a gun mounted on top and snapped at the driver to follow the land–rover. Thorwald and the others commandeered a jeep and joined the chase. The stillness of the night was shattered as a whole convoy of trucks and jeeps took off after the escaped S.K.U.N.K. agents.

They raced down the road towards the south. They passed the jeep they'd abandoned when they'd escaped from the radar station that morning. The gap between the landrover and the pursuing vehicles was narrowing...

Then Olga turned off the road and they followed her along a rutted track. At a bend in the track, the landrover suddenly disappeared. When they arrived at the same place, Aisling saw what had happened: the track descended quite steeply to, she could hardly believe it, the little cove where the *Fafnir* was bobbing up and down peacefully alongside the pier.

The sun had sunk completely now and the long northern twilight had begun. A curtain of rain was sweeping across the sea towards them—the sky was black with the approaching storm. In the poor light, it was hard to see what was happening. Aisling strained her eyes.

She saw Olga stop the landrover at the very edge of the pier, within inches of the water. Three figures jumped out of the landrover and into the ship. Shavitov single-handedly raised the mast and set the huge red and white sail. Olga cast off. A puff of wind filled the sail and the *Fafnir* began to move away from the jetty. They were going to escape!

Hansie had stopped his vehicle on the track just above the shed they'd been locked into that morning. He scrambled onto the roof of the car. There was a flash and a deafening roar. The shadow that was the *Fafnir* seemed to quiver. Hansie fired the mortar again. This time a bright flash illuminated the shattered mast. Flames licked at the red and white sail. Aisling could see the black shadows of Olga and the two men trying to put out the blaze.

Hansie fired once more. No shadows moved now on the shattered deck. They watched in silence as the flames engulfed the proud dragon head. Ablaze from stem to stern, the *Fafnir* sailed slowly out to sea.

Chris put his hand on Aisling's shoulder. His fingers bit into her flesh until she squealed. He didn't hear her. He stared at the burning ship, his face white, tears running down his cheeks.

"It is better so, my friend," said Thorwald quietly. "Death must come to us all one day. And she has had the funeral of a Viking chief." His voice was calm although his face was sad. Aisling felt for him: she knew how he cared about his ship. He put his arm round Erik's shoulders. "She was a good ship," he said simply. "She has given herself for a good cause. We must not grieve too much."

Hansie jumped down from the mortar and came over to them. He looked at their dazed faces.

"I am sorry about the *Fafnir*, Thorwald. But I had to do it. Yourself and Archie there will get another ship one day, I am sure."

"Nae me," Archie said. "I'm gaein' back tae Ireland wi' Florence. Her and me, we're getting married." He blushed a scarlet that would have put the most brilliant sunset to shame.

Aisling couldn't believe her ears. "But you're both far too..." *Old,* she was going to say, but a warning glance from John Smith stopped her just in time.

Hansie laughed. "Come," he said. "Let us go back to Florence and Seamus. If we don't tell Seamus soon what's happening, his temper will be such as to start another volcano all on his own. And your cat, Aisling, will no doubt be waiting to be fed."

Aisling couldn't help smiling. Hansie grinned encouragingly. "And then you will all come back to Reykjavik with me. Your welcome in Iceland has not been typical—it is time you enjoyed some Icelandic hospitality."

"Are Helga and Igmar safe?" Thorwald asked.

"Yes, thanks be to God. My men tell me that they have found them both and that they are unharmed."

"Hansie's wife and daughter were kidnapped by S.K.U.N.K. That was why he had to agree to go with them to meet the *Fafnir*," John Smith explained to Aisling.

Hansie looked at Chris, who was still staring sadly out at the darkening sea. "Come and meet Helga, Christopher. She is nineteen and blond and, although a father may be prejudiced, there is no doubt but that she is beautiful too."

The tragic expression left Chris's face. "Is she?" he asked enthusiastically. "How long will it take to get there?"

Not too long, Aisling hoped. What she wanted more than anything else right now was a bath. And then John Smith would find her a seat on a plane back to Dublin.

Intrepid Irish schoolgirl risks her life to save the world! Next time, she'd have more sense and stay at home.

*Irish Myths and Tales for
Young People*
by
Carolyn Swift

This new collection contains fourteen ancient
Irish tales, told so that young readers can enjoy
all their heroism and treachery, magic and
romance, fun and foolishness. There are tales of
daring athletes and boastful champions, beautiful girls changed into butterflies or fawns, wise
women who outwit armies, murderous kings,
wicked step-mothers, one-eyed giants, sinister
druids and mysterious sea voyages. All play
their part in this enthralling kaleidoscope of
Irish legends.

Children's
POOLBEG

The Long March
by
Michael Mullen

After the battle of Kinsale, on the last day of the year 1602, O'Sullivan Beare left Glengarriff in County Cork with one thousand followers, the remnants of a race defeated by the English in a cruel war. They set out to reach the safety of O'Rourke's castle in Leitrim. Two weeks later only thirty-five people reached their goal. The rest had perished on the way or abandoned the march.

Michael Mullen recreates one of the most re-markable episodes in Irish history in this grip-ping and stirring novel for young readers.

Children's
POOLBEG

A Likely Story
by
Mary Lavin

Packy is the only son of a poor widow and they
live in a tumbledown cottage in Ireland. He has
heard whispers of Little People and gold hoards
and changelings. His mother dismisses these
tales as "likely stories" but Packy is not so sure.
For some time he thinks he has seen out of the
corner of his eye a beckoning hand. Then, one
day, on his way home from school he meets a
mysterious little man...

This is a story, likely or not, that will keep you
reading to the end.

Children's
POOLBEG

Robbers on TV
by
Carolyn Swift

Maura, Whacker and May find intrigue
in the television studios and behind the
scenes.

Children's
POOLBEG